ALSO BY STEPHANIE GREY

The Immortal Prudence Blackwood
A Witchly Influence

ZOMBIE RESPONSE TEAM

ZRT

DIVISION TENNESSEE
A NOVEL

STEPHANIE GREY

bhc
press™

Livonia, Michigan

Editor: Lana King
Proofreader: Keera Lydon

ZRT: DIVISION TENNESSEE

Copyright © 2021 Stephanie Grey

This book is a work of fiction. The characters, incidents, and dialogue are drawn from the author's imagination and are not to be construed as real. Any resemblance to actual events or persons, living or dead, is entirely coincidental.

Published by BHC Press

Library of Congress Control Number: 2020950329

ISBN: 978-1-64397-270-1 (Hardcover)
ISBN: 978-1-64397-271-8 (Softcover)
ISBN: 978-1-64397-272-5 (Ebook)

For information, write:
BHC Press
885 Penniman #5505
Plymouth, MI 48170

Visit the publisher:
www.bhcpress.com

For Grandma Thomas, who would've greatly disliked this type of book because it's not exactly a Hallmark movie, but would have been proud of me for writing it regardless.

ZRT: DIVISION TENNESSEE

PROLOGUE

THREE YEARS AGO

Elisabeth Mayfair scurried up the concrete wall with their supplies. After tossing the bags to the yard on the other side, she reached down to help her twin sister, Margo, pull herself up. The horde that had been chasing them caught up and grabbed Margo's foot. They violently yanked her down, and without thinking, Elisabeth jumped from the top of the wall and began swinging the ax that she always carried. The more decomposed undead lost their heads quickly; the fresher ones were only partially decapitated. She felt a pinch on her right shoulder blade but kept swinging until she saw Margo had safely gotten up the wall.

Elisabeth hurled her ax over the barrier and climbed quickly. "What?" she asked.

"There's blood on you," Margo replied. Her face was wet with tears.

"Yes, some of the fresher ones still have liquid blood."

"No, Lizzy. It's *your* blood." The sisters climbed down to their side of the wall, and Margo gingerly lifted Elisabeth's shirt, gasping at the bite wound. "We'll clean it and maybe kill the infection in time. We can cauterize it."

Elisabeth shook her head. "No. You need to shoot me. I don't want to become one of them." Margo frowned and shook her head slowly. "For God's sake, Margo, I'll do it myself." She stormed away to her room, passing her mother sitting quietly in the den. The window was open; her mother had heard everything. She made no move to stop her daughter.

Elisabeth grasped her gun tightly, her hand trembling. Margo filled the doorway, her arms folded. "What are you doing? Move. I'm going to the woods so you won't have me rotting here."

"Oh, Lizzy," Margo said softly. "Always so strong. I wonder if you're strong enough to survive this." Quickly, Margo pulled the door shut and locked it with a skeleton key.

SEVEN DAYS PASSED, and Elisabeth heard the door unlock slowly.

Margo was on point, though her 9mm weapon wavered slightly. Their mother lingered behind her, a shotgun firmly pressed against her shoulder and her finger on the trigger. Margo opened the door, and let out a small cry of surprise to find Elisabeth curled up on her bed, her eyes crimson.

"Either shoot me or get me something to drink," Elisabeth demanded.

Their mother dropped to her knees, the shotgun clattering to the floor as tears cascaded freely down her cheeks while she prayed.

Margo cautiously approached Elisabeth, her palms clammy. "Lizzy?"

Elisabeth sat up and swung her legs over the bed. She took off her shirt so that her sister could see her back. The bite mark was now a faint scar.

Margo rushed toward her sister and embraced her tightly. "Oh, my God, Lizzy! I'm so happy you're alive! I knew you could make it! I knew you'd be a survivor! We thought those were just rumors, but I'm so thankful the rumors were true this time!"

Uncomfortable with the overwhelming sense of emotion, Elisabeth opened her mouth to speak.

"No, Lizzy!" Margo screamed. She raised her gun and fired.

"Fuck, Margo!" Elisabeth shouted. She placed her hand over her stomach, blood seeping between her fingers.

Margo dropped her weapon and put her own hands over Elisabeth's wound to add pressure. "I thought you were going to bite me! I'm so sorry!" she said with a sob.

The blood was already clotting. "What in the hell?" the twins asked in unison. Elisabeth raised her shirt for the second time that morning and watched the wound close. She leaned forward, and the exit wound was already healed. "You were lucky that was a clean through and through shot," she said warily. "I don't know if I would have survived having a bullet in me."

Margo laughed uneasily. "We need to figure out what other kind of super powers you have."

ONE

"**E**xcuse me, ma'am, but there's a zombie walking around the shoe department."

"Thank you. I'll take care of it right away." Libby Porter sighed as the customer hastily walked out of the store. Those damn zombies would never go away. Three years after the war—battle, really—and you could still find them wandering around the world. Some poor creature would get bitten and wake up a week later as a zombie. Symptoms? Ha! Waking up as a zombie is a pretty good symptom pointing toward your new condition.

Libby flipped her long, dark hair over her shoulder and reached for the phone. She dialed 917.

"Zombie Hotline. How may we help you today?" quipped a crisp female voice.

"Hi, my name is Libby Porter. I work at Bella Couture and we have a zombie in the shoe department. Oh, no. Scratch that. He's gone over to the accessories department."

"Are there people around?"

Libby snorted. "Of course there are."

A pause. "Ma'am, why haven't you cleared the area? Zombies are still dangerous. You need to make an announcement immediately and clear the area. A team is already on their way."

"Whatever, lady. Just get me some damn guns here, okay?" Libby hung up the phone. Who did that woman think she was? She wasn't going to clear out the store because of one zombie. People could still browse and enjoy their shopping experience. A little bit of a stench and the small threat of a zombie's quick lunge if you get too close wasn't so bad. Just don't be an idiot and get too close! The economy was still getting back on its feet, and she wasn't about to lose her commission. Libby had her eye on the new turquoise necklace that had recently arrived, and she leaned over the counter to peer down into its sparkling beauty.

Lost in her thoughts, Libby didn't notice the zombie had moved again. The smell of rot assaulted her and she wrinkled her nose in disgust. Looking up, she saw the zombie was now just across the counter and growling at her. "Oh, shove off you piece of decay." Libby backed away from the counter and walked toward the exit from her area and into the rest of the store, her four-inch heels clicking against the floor. The zombie had already moved to block her way. "Son of a bitch!" she shouted. "Someone please help me!" She frantically looked around, but there wasn't a customer in sight.

Libby reached out and grabbed a fist full of diamond bracelets dangling from their display and slid them over her knuckles. She cocked her arm back and, with all of her might, punched the zombie in the face.

Confused, the zombie staggered back and Libby bolted toward the main exit.

Men in battle gear charged through the entrance. "It's about damn time!" Libby shouted. She shook off the bracelets and noticed a cut on her hand.

A tall woman with chestnut hair stepped into the store, her mouth moving rapidly as she gave orders through her throat mic. Finally, she noticed Libby standing nearby. "Libby Porter," the woman said, her voice steady and not questioning to whom she was speaking.

Libby felt herself stand up straighter. "Yes."

"You reported a zombie to dispatch seventeen minutes ago."

Libby nodded. "I did. He's…" Libby trailed off. She wasn't sure where the zombie had gone.

The woman eyed Libby's wounded hand and started reaching into her wrist cuff. "How did you get cut?"

"I punched the zombie in the face."

"Did you have any protection?"

Libby pointed to the diamond bracelets on the floor. "Yes, I put those over my knuckles."

The woman nodded and yanked a syringe out of her wrist cuff. "You've mixed blood with the infected. This will help." She grabbed Libby's arm and turned her wrist so that it was facing up. "This will sting a little," she warned. Quickly, she plunged the needle into Libby's soft flesh and Libby heard herself sigh for the second time that day. Her knees buckled and the chestnut-haired woman gently caught her and helped her to a comfortable sitting position on the floor. Libby leaned forward, her head resting on her hands until sleep overwhelmed her and she fell onto her side.

ELISABETH MAYFAIR WATCHED Libby Porter die peacefully. She pressed her fingers to Libby's neck to be sure, then removed her gun from her holster and shot Libby between her eyes.

"Jesus, did you have to shoot her in the face?"

"Yes, I did, Rhys. You know the protocol."

Rhys Corben frowned, his dark brown eyebrows knitting together.

"Was she even infected?"

Rhys and Elisabeth turned to face the voice that was, despite numerous throat lozenges, destined to be scratchy. "Yes," Elisabeth replied.

Dallas Anderson stepped closer and put his left boot onto Libby's wrist, rolling it so that he could see her knuckles. He inhaled sharply. "You determined she was infected without a field test? It isn't possible to tell from a wound this small," Dallas snapped. "You could've stabbed her through her brain stem so that it wouldn't have marked her face for the funeral."

Rhys snorted. "You're wrong. You know Elisabeth is an Abnormal."

Dallas narrowed his pale blue eyes. "Oh, yes, the lady in charge is in that role because she's an Abnormal."

"You're on the cleanup team, Dallas. Dispose of this body properly. We'll discuss your attitude when we get back."

Amelia Stone slapped Dallas on his back. "Come on, cowboy. Tuck your tail between your legs and let's clean up the mess." She turned and winked at Elisabeth over her shoulder.

Elisabeth watched Amelia lead Dallas away to gather the cleanup supplies from their vehicle. Usually, there was a specific crew to take care of the bodies, but they were all out at other sites. A thought flickered briefly that there was a potential, unmentioned outbreak, but it was quickly dismissed. While the members of the Zombie Response Team, or ZRT, weren't military by any means, she knew that information like that would be out in the open and never a secret. Secrets like that were too dangerous to the public. Half of the world's population had been lost because the original government didn't want to scare people. What they didn't realize is that an unprepared population is unpredictable and, quite frankly, scared shitless when some walking undead thing comes charging into their living rooms during an episode of a late-night talk show.

Her own team was strong, despite their occasional disputes. They had all signed up because they had lost people they loved and, now that the war was almost over, wanted to make sure another outbreak didn't happen. When she had taken over almost a year ago, she had promised them transparency and that she'd die herself before she let anything happen to one of them.

Elisabeth spoke quietly with the manager of Bella Couture, apologizing for the mess she had created. She was grateful for his positive attitude and that he wasn't upset. The manager shook her hand and thanked her once more for ZRT's swift response before walking away, already on the phone trying to find a replacement for Libby Porter.

THE TEAM HAD returned to The Creamery, the affectionate term given to the crematorium ZRT used as its headquarters. It had added a very comfortable office space with spacious, cushy offices for its team leaders. Having a crematorium onsite to dispose of the bodies was extremely convenient. It definitely beat the days when they had to bury each one. There were the cases where the family wanted the body for a funeral service, but some families didn't want the negative stigma of a zombie in their bloodline and paid ZRT to dispose of them quietly.

"I want to know how in the hell a zombie made it to the mall without anyone noticing," Rhys said, removing his black body armor.

"He was fairly fresh," Dallas answered. He began breaking down his Ruger AR-556 to clean. "I suppose people saw him and just thought he was homeless. No one is going to stop a homeless guy from going into a mall."

"What about the smell? You can notice the smell of a zombie. No, don't look at me like that, Dallas. They all have a stench."

"What all has a stench?" Elisabeth asked, joining the rest of her team in the locker room. She began to remove her own weapons and armor.

Rhys paused and eyed Elisabeth carefully. She was absently stroking the small hatchet she carried. He cleared his throat nervously. He wasn't about to tell Elisabeth that, as an Abnormal, she had an odd scent that he couldn't quite place. Fresh dirt, maybe?

"He's talking about the zombie smell," Amelia answered. She glanced quickly at Rhys as if she had done him a favor.

"Oh." Elisabeth nodded in agreement. "They do. I know I must." She watched as her team looked everywhere in the room but at her. "Guys, stop it. I know I smell. I just hope I don't stink. Comes with the territory of everything else we get after being bitten."

"I don't care how they smell. I'm shooting them. Every single one," Dallas said. His weapon was in pieces on the table in front of him, his cleaning supplies lovingly laid out next to it.

Elisabeth's head snapped in Dallas' direction. "I thought you preferred to sever the brain stem and keep their faces intact," she said coldly.

The rest of the team froze as Dallas reddened. "She's got a family," he said quietly.

"You can start doing that for the next Libby Porter," Elisabeth replied. She gazed over her team. "Don't question me again in the field when it comes to whether or not people are zombies. I can literally smell it on them, and feel the virus coursing underneath their skin when I touch them. Do you understand?"

Dallas nodded.

"Get dressed. You have reports to turn in."

When Elisabeth left the locker room, Rhys burped loudly. "Sorry," he said sheepishly. "Awkwardness makes me gassy."

Amelia laughed and slipped her cream silk blouse over her head. "Better out your mouth than your ass."

ELISABETH TAPPED HER pen thoughtfully against her chin. Rhys had asked a good question earlier: how *had* that zombie made it into the mall undetected? She had heard her team talking amongst themselves before they were aware of her presence. Eavesdropping hadn't always been a habit of hers, but she had found it could be useful. As the war came to a close and society tried to piece itself back together, people climbing the ladder had a nasty habit of claiming they had plans to lead everyone else. The truth, she learned, was that they had an outline and they were basically all the same: eliminate the enemy, which, in this case, was the rest of the zombies. Elisabeth wasn't sure if they'd ever actually get all of the zombies; the world was just too big with too many hiding places and too many areas that remained third world countries with few resources. With the United States unable to spare any extra soldiers, it couldn't continue to be the world police and the rest of NATO had had to step up and become more active in solving the pandemic.

When the news of Abnormals hit, the military immediately tried to shut down the so-called "rumors." People were desperate. People were stupid. They tried chaining up their loved ones or locking them in a room like Elisabeth herself had been in the hope that they somehow carried the gene that bonded with the virus. The odds of actually bonding were astronomical, and Elisabeth didn't know anyone else like herself. Oh, they existed, that she was sure of. She wished she could meet them so that she could compare which abilities had been gained. Were they each different, or were they all the same? Either way, Abnormals were commodities and usually placed as leaders for eradication teams. Zombie Response Team was all over the United States, and Elisabeth couldn't imagine it being an entity that ever vanished. She knew there were other companies throughout the world that were similar to ZRT, but they were smaller and less organized.

The zombie that had entered the mall had been fairly fresh. Its clothes weren't tattered and its hair wasn't too askew. It couldn't have come from very far away. Sometimes, people took a trip somewhere remote where the certainty of clearance wasn't one hundred percent and came back infected unknowingly. She'd had Research do some digging to unearth the zombie's whereabouts. His name was Jasper Tonks, and he had been a financial advisor.

Elisabeth frowned. Libby Porter didn't have to die. She supposed she didn't have to shoot her in the head, but that was the most efficient way of ensuring that a future zombie stayed dead. She didn't distrust the serum that she carried with her, but a bullet scrambling the brain helped her sleep better at night. Elisabeth had begged ZRT to have mandatory classes on how to handle the zombies if encountered, but they firmly told her no. Letting her anger get the best of her, Elisabeth had smashed her hand on the conference table and it broke in half, crumpling inward.

"Damn it, Ethan, the public needs to learn how not to be a bunch of idiots!"

Ethan Brown didn't flinch. "The people aren't 'idiots,'" he replied calmly. "This war is fresh on their minds and they are well aware of the consequences of getting too close to the infected. What we need to keep everything rolling smoothly is for the public to feel secure and safe in their daily lives the way they did prewar."

"What you're saying translates to you want them to have a false sense of security so that, over time, they will become more complacent and unable to defend themselves. Ethan, those gun rights activists are already starting to crawl out of the woodwork and we all know it was the ones with the guns that saved our asses in the first place. Call them rednecks if you will, but those men and women saved a lot of lives with their hidden arsenals."

Ethan shook his head. "This discussion is over, Elisabeth." He leaned closer and almost whispered to her. "I'd drop it if I were you. Just because you're an Abnormal doesn't mean you won't get put down. You're still technically infected with the virus and we don't know if you can pass it on or not. Be lucky your kind haven't been herded and turned into lab experiments."

Elisabeth raised her chin defiantly. "Are you threatening me?"

The head of ZRT Division Tennessee simply stared evenly at the Abnormal until quickly turning on his heel and exiting the room. Over his shoulder, he said casually, "You owe us a new table."

"I have our reports for you, ma'am," Rhys said, pulling Elisabeth out of her reverie. He stepped into Elisabeth's office and held out the proffered paperwork.

Elisabeth took them and skimmed over them. "These are fine. You can take them to Tammy for filing."

Tammy Goodwin was the office manager and receptionist. She was also the source of Rhys' affections, which were ignored.

Rhys smiled. "I wonder if she's busy later."

"I'm sure she is."

"Maybe the fiftieth time is the charm."

Elisabeth chuckled. "You won't be able to wear her down, you know. Isn't it a bit cliché to like the receptionist?"

Rhys' mouth widened in mock shock. "Is it? I had no idea. I have only seen the films where it's the boss and the secretary, not the colleague and the secretary."

"Get out of here," Elisabeth said, a grin on her face.

Rhys Corben left Elisabeth's office, reports in hand. He liked the new team leader. The previous leader had transferred to Division Virginia. When his team was briefed that Elisabeth Mayfair was an Abnormal, he was stunned. Like most, he assumed they were a rumor, something to inspire hope amongst the dwindling population. Her red eyes were unsettling in the beginning, but he was used to them now. When new people met her, they were unnerved. While her condition was meant to be a secret, she never bothered to hide them. People had been exposed to zombies, so why wouldn't a person having red eyes be unbelievable?

He hummed quietly to himself as he made his way to Tammy Goodwin's desk. He stepped into a cubicle and watched her for a moment, taking in her beauty. She had a soft brown pixie cut and brown eyes to match. Her skin was creamy, and while she was no scrawny woman, she was clearly strong and athletic. Rhys knew she had grown up on a farm and worked hard until it was lost, burned to the ground, during the war. Some of her family were still on the land trying to resurrect it to its former glory, but Tammy decided to move to the city instead and start over.

"Don't quit your day job," Tammy said. She was shuffling papers around on her desk, trying to organize them into the multiple stacking trays she had.

"You know you love my voice," Rhys retorted. Tammy had a counter that surrounded her desk, reminding him of a bar, and he leaned over it casually.

"I love it when your voice stops talking." Tammy didn't even bother to look up. "Just leave the reports there and I'll take care of them."

Rhys sighed and looked around quickly. Lowering his voice, he said, "Tammy, I really do like you."

Tammy paused and met his gaze with her own.

Rhys felt like his heart was skipping a beat and he waited for her to reply.

Instead, Tammy laughed. "Rhys! I almost believed you! Look, I know your type. You're cute. You're charming. You're a little boyish and all of the ladies want you and you have them at will. I've seen those families that come in that want us to remove zombies quietly so as not to tarnish their good names. You woo the young women, flash those baby blues, get what you want, and you move onto the next poor victim."

Rhys raised a finger. "I appreciate your compliment, but to be fair, the next victim is the wrong choice of words. Let's be sensitive here. A victim is the person who got turned into a zombie. The casualties are the people who are left behind to pick up the pieces."

Tammy's lips were pursed. "You're not helping your cause. Get out of my space."

"Seems to be the consensus of the day," Rhys replied, admitting defeat. To Tammy's annoyance, he started humming again as he walked back to his cubicle.

Hours later, Elisabeth left The Creamery long after everyone else on her team departed. There were other teams with whom they shared the office space, but their schedules overlapped to accommodate twenty-four-hour coverage. She waved goodbye to the members of Team Aguilar. Some were still gathered in the kitchen getting their caffeine fix and merely mumbled in response. She didn't mind; it was early morning for them.

Elisabeth pulled out her bicycle. Cars had just become available merely a year before once the refineries and deliveries were running again, but she seldom drove. She lived close to the office and there was a company SUV that they drove to assignments. She was a hypocrite, though. Had she known anyone else that rode a bike around after dark, she would chastise them immediately. It just wasn't safe, despite what Ethan Brown and the other leaders of ZRT wanted people to believe. She was an Abnormal, though. Zombies didn't attack her anyway.

The power for the streetlights was out again when she reached her suburb. That was becoming a more common occurrence as the electrical company worked out the kinks with the nearby dam. They had been warned it would happen, at least. Her neighborhood was adjacent to a small forest, and while Elisabeth didn't worry about herself, she did worry about her neighbors. She'd rather look outside and be able to see potential threats than guess their presence.

Nearing her house, she passed a small group of three women in their mid-twenties—close to Elisabeth's age—and waved. They waved back and smiled.

Parking her bike in her garage, she heard a scream. Alert, she stood rigid, listening to pinpoint the origin. Another scream followed and Elisabeth double-checked the Smith and Wesson 9mm she always holstered before darting toward the sound.

Quickly, she came upon the group of women she had passed moments ago and saw a large man holding one of their wrists. The other two were too terrified to move as they watched the attacker bring his face closer to their friend. Elisabeth ducked, one knee hitting the ground as she grabbed the man around his waist and tackled him. She scrambled and sat on his stomach, her knees splayed out for balance and her chest close to his. She weighed more than she looked, and the man grunted underneath the pressure of her body on top of his.

Already knowing the answer, Elisabeth leaned close and sniffed. "Motherfucker," she said, exhaling heavily. He reached his arms around her as if to hug her, but she bucked upward, breaking his grip. She pressed her hands onto his sternum to pop herself up and, grabbing the back of his arm with her right hand, swung her left leg over his head. She was now in a T-shape next to him, legs over his chest, his right arm held close to her body. She lifted her hips and the man began to yell in pain. His elbow was bending backward, and Elisabeth was perfectly content to break it.

"Wait!" shouted one of the women.

Elisabeth didn't listen and broke the man's arm. The crack was sickening and one of the women immediately vomited.

"You bitch!" spat the man. "You broke my arm!"

Elisabeth stood and calmly brushed off her shirt. "You should get that checked out, sir. I would also suggest that you reconsider your decision to attack people in the future."

"Joey!" cried the smallest woman, the one whose wrists he had been holding. She angrily glared at Elisabeth. "It was just a prank!" she cried.

"It was a stupid prank."

"I can't believe she broke your arm, baby," sobbed the woman. "Come on, we'll get it fixed." She helped the man to his feet. Turning back to Elisabeth, she said, "You better watch your back, you crazy bitch. We were just having fun."

Elisabeth glanced at the other women. They were still shaking; clearly, the world wasn't ready for scary pranks. "Get serious, woman!" Elisabeth yelled. "Have you forgotten who you're talking to now? I just broke his arm because I considered him a threat. Do you really think I'll hesitate to harm you if I feel threatened?"

The woman cast her eyes downward and Elisabeth walked back toward her home.

"I see you've made some new friends."

Elisabeth hung up her holster on the coat stand by her front door. "If you're foolish enough to pull a stupid prank like that, you deserve to be punished. The war is all but over, but it's still too soon to pretend to attack anyone and call it a prank. That wasn't even acceptable prewar."

Margo Mayfair uncrossed her legs and rose from the oversized sage-green chair. "He was a human, wasn't he?" she asked.

Elisabeth knew the lecture was coming. She just nodded.

"You can't do that and you know it. ZRT will have your ass for hurting civilians, whether they deserve it or not," she scolded. "You knew damn good and well he was just a human. You probably knew when you laid eyes on him."

"I did," Elisabeth finally said. "They'll think twice the next time they want to play a prank. Pranks are supposed to be funny, aren't they? Why not put saran wrap under the toilet seat so the next person who uses it makes a big mess?"

Margo pretended to gag. "That's disgusting, Lizzy."

"Like you never did that to Jimmy after you found out he kissed Veronica underneath the bleachers."

Margo's face cracked into a wide grin. "Oh, I did do that, didn't I? I wonder how those two are."

"Zombies in Division Louisiana."

"Really?"

"Yeah, that hurricane came through and uprooted a bunch of coffins. The vaults were wrenched open, the caskets exposed, and all of those people whose families thought they just buried someone indefinitely came back wanting to eat everyone. ZRT called in teams from all over the South to help put the genie back into the bottle."

"But they were buried together?" Margo asked.

"Supposedly. Young love, world going to chaos, and parents thinking they were doing what was best for their kids."

"Aww, that's sweet. Well, look at who's a dead zombie now and who's still human." Margo twirled in place, her laugh reminding Elisabeth of gentle wind chimes. When was she done, she added, "By the way, Mom sent over some leftovers."

Elisabeth's stomach began to growl in response. She couldn't remember the last time she had eaten. Opening the refrigerator, she was suddenly ravenous. "How is Mom?" she asked, pulling out a large casserole dish.

"She's fine. She wants you to move back in with us. The new house is great. They build them now so that they're fortified already and they have separate living quarters to accommodate growing families who still want to live under one roof."

Elisabeth's oven beeped its readiness and she popped in the casserole to reheat. "People in other countries have been sharing much smaller homes long before the war ever came along," she pointed out.

Margo snorted. "This is America. Home of excess. Not so much anymore because of the war, but people will go back to their old ways within the next ten years. Look at how far we've come in just three short years."

"Do you really think that's the case? I think there was too much loss for people to return to the days where they practically worshipped families only famous because one of their daughters fucked some guy on a leaked porno."

"I liked that show!" Margo exclaimed.

Dragging her casserole out of the oven, Elisabeth said, "Of course you did."

"It was entertainment. You, on the other hand, wanted to watch *Forensic Files* all of the time."

With her mouth full, Elisabeth replied, "You can learn from that show."

"Don't be gross, Lizzy," Margo complained. "Besides, you can kill all you want now and no one will ever say a word to you. You don't have to worry about evidence."

"Those people are already dead."

"Some aren't even zombies yet and you still kill them." Margo's tone had turned serious.

Each twin stood on separate sides in the galley kitchen, staring at each other. Slowly, Elisabeth swallowed and put her plate on the counter. "It's better that they're dead before they wake up a week later as a zombie. They're still doing research to see how infectious they are before they make the actual turn. I don't just eliminate them, Margo. I eliminate the possibly of it spreading. If you haven't noticed, we haven't won the war yet. We'll have won when all zombies are gone and so is the virus."

"Lizzy, do you know what you're saying?" Margo asked quietly. "They're doing research on your kind to see if you're infectious and, if the virus has to die, then so do you."

"They're not doing research on Abnormals."

"Now who's being an idiot? What, did your director tell you that? He probably did just to pacify you. Don't be so naïve. They're not going to let a bunch of people with mutated genes wander around leading eradication teams and, for those who aren't part of ZRT, just hang out with the general population without knowing *something*."

Elisabeth was silent.

"Don't you ever worry that, one day, they're going to take us both and research us because we're identical twins? I would if I were them. One twin was exposed and became an Abnormal. Would the same happen to the other twin? Is it really in the genes like they assume? Or is it something special, as unique to us as our souls?"

"Margo, knock it off. They already know the virus bonds with a gene, which does mutate it. I'd be surprised if you got bitten and the same didn't happen to you. Quit being like one of those people who believes in conspiracy theories."

Margo bit the bottom of her lip. She was about to cry. "No, you knock it off! Those scientists don't know for sure. Do you really think three years is enough to know? They just came out with the best, most logical explanation to soothe and reassure everyone. They even named the gene as proof, but I think that was mostly to back up their claims."

Elisabeth put her hands on Margo's shoulders. "Listen to me," she said sternly. "You have to stop this line of conversation. Most people think Abnormals are a rumor anyway, so it doesn't matter, does it? My own team was surprised to learn of my condition because even they thought it wasn't real. Most people think it was just something created to give them hope. You know better than anyone that the real Abnormals have been sworn to secrecy and so have their families. If any experiments were going to happen, they would have happened already. You're right: research does take a long time. But genes were being identified so often and so easily pinpointed that there was less and less 'junk DNA' and uses for each were being discovered." Elisabeth hugged her sister. "It's okay. It will continue to be okay."

Margo sniffed. "I just worry about you so much. Mom worries, too." She sniffed again.

"Are you getting snot in my hair?"

"A little."

JESSICA LARS ANGRILY slammed the car door and huffed as she walked to the passenger side to let out Joey, her boyfriend of seven months. She couldn't believe that her bitch neighbor had broken his arm! She always knew that woman had been a little weird. There was something about her, though, that made Jessica a little afraid and comforted by her presence at the same time.

Joey Stephens yawned, groggy from the drugs given to him at the hospital. They had lied and said they were robbed to avoid any possible issues. The nurse had clucked her tongue disapprovingly and said, "Don't we have enough problems these days?" Jessica had just nodded in agreement as she snatched away the clipboard and began to fill out Joey's information.

"Babe, that was a stupid idea. I don't know why I wanted to scare your friends." Joey slung his good arm around Jessica's shoulders.

"It's not just your fault. I thought it would be funny, too." Jessica grunted under his weight as they walked toward the front door. She fumbled for her keys while trying to hold up her boyfriend.

"We'll get her back."

"Get who back, Joey?"

"The bitch who did this to me," Joey said, his words slurred.

Jessica shoved the key into the lock and cranked it to the left. "Don't be ridiculous, Joey," she said, her voice firm. "You can talk all you want, but we can't actually do anything to her. You saw her skills. We can't match that."

Joey let his girlfriend haul him to the sofa where he sat down heavily. She went back to lock the door behind her. "I don't have to deal with her directly. I can shoot her."

Silence.

"Did you hear me? I said I'd shoot the bitch! See, babe, no problem." He grinned to himself.

"No, you can't hurt her. She's too important."

"What did you say, Jessica? You taking her side now after what she did to me?"

A dark figure entered the living room. Joey squinted, trying to make out who it was. "What are you doing in my house?" he demanded.

Suddenly, his head jolted backward, brain matter spraying the back of the couch, the wall, and part of the ceiling.

The figure stepped over Jessica's body as it exited the home. She looked like she was sleeping except that her neck was at an impossible angle.

The figure paused, then closed the door behind it to shutter the neighbors against the horror inside.

TWO

A melia Stone scooped her long, auburn hair into her hands and wrapped a hair tie haphazardly around it to create a ponytail. Hair off her face, she put on her wireless headphones and stuffed her phone in her back pocket. It took a little over a year for the Internet to return and for cellular phone service to be restored. People can say what they want about the government, but they really did light a fire under everyone's ass to get society close to where it had been before zombies started devouring the living. Things weren't quite the same as they had been, and they probably never would be, but Amelia was fine with that. She'd always been a little quirky and a bit of an outcast. Being alone had never bothered her, and during the war she had spent a lot of time on her own wandering from place to place and helping those in need. She wasn't special like Elisabeth Mayfair, but she was an even better shot than comic book superheroes and wasn't scared easily.

Her first encounter with a zombie had left her virtually unfazed. Amelia had been at the gun range shooting one of her favorite weapons: a Kimber Stainless Gold Match II. She loved its weight, its accuracy. It had been a great day so far. There were two employees behind the counter and three patrons a few lanes down from her. Two of the people were obviously a couple and Amelia had laughed as she walked by the woman. She had been wearing heels and a low-cut shirt on this particular date. She shot Amelia a nasty glare as she passed and Amelia had simply shrugged in response.

It wasn't too long before the woman began screeching, "Ouch! That's hot!" Amelia laughed again. Heels were not meant to be worn at the range and a low-cut shirt was just begging for hot, spent shells to fall down between breasts. Amelia's parents, both police officers, had taught her well. Close-toed shoes, hair back, crewneck shirt, jeans. *That* was the appropriate attire for the gun range.

She fired the last of her ammunition and decided to call it a day. "What's up, Lou?" she said casually as she paid for her time in the lane.

Lou grunted.

"Lou, don't talk so much! Listen, you see that live one in there with Ned? Fifth one he's brought here this week. Man needs to come up with a better filter for finding a good one."

"He doesn't care about finding a 'good one.' Just someone dumb enough to think he's manly and will go to bed with him." Lou held out his hand waiting for Amelia's credit card, the harsh lighting bouncing off his bald, shiny head.

"Then I think I just busted his balls because I'm a better shot than him any day."

"You a dyke?"

"No." Amelia handed Lou her payment.

"Then why do you care what he does?"

"I don't. I was just making conversation."

Lou swiped Amelia's card and returned it. "Whatever, Amelia. I'll see you next week."

Amelia nodded and turned to leave. She spotted another woman sitting in the lobby, her head down against her chest. Amelia jabbed her thumb toward the woman. "Lou, who's that broad with?"

"She came in with that other guy that was in there with you. Said she wasn't interested in shooting and I think she's asleep now."

"Wish I could sleep like that," Amelia murmured. She pushed open the front door and stepped into the snow storm that had found its way into the Appalachian Mountains. She loved the snow, the way it swirled before it hit the ground. The panic of the locals always gave her a chuckle because they all behaved like they'd never seen the white, powdery substance before and drove slower than a tortoise.

Popping open her trunk, she tossed in her gear and briefly remembered that she had left her carry permit at the house, but it wasn't a big deal. Tennessee had already passed a law that allowed its residents to carry guns in their cars and in their offices without the need for a carry permit. *God bless this state and its people,* Amelia thought.

Amelia slammed the trunk shut, and as her hand reached the door handle, she heard very distinctive *pops*. She shouldn't have been able to hear that sound this clearly in the middle of a snow storm if people were shooting in the separate range. Whistling a tune whose name she couldn't remember, she opened her trunk again and fished out the Kimber. She grabbed the extra magazine she kept hidden in the compartment where her spare tire was and slammed it into place. Still whistling, Amelia went back into the building.

Inside she found chaos. The sleeping woman had woken and was eating Lou. She'd either put a lot of him away already or she was just making a mess. Peering closer, Amelia realized the woman was just a sloppy eater. She checked the range and saw that the three people who had shared the lanes with her had locked themselves inside. The other employee—his name tag read *Sawyer*—was slumped over on the ground. Amelia leaned down and checked him, rolling her eyes at his hair that he had carefully styled into a casually messy bun. His clothes screamed "hipster" and she shook her head. When she didn't find any marks on him and decided he had passed out from fear, she grabbed a pair of scissors off the counter and cut his hair to a length she felt acceptable. "Serves you right for letting poor Lou get eaten. Honestly, you work at a gun range that rents out guns and sells ammo. You should look more respectable."

Standing up, scissors still in hand, she shouted, "Hey, lady!" The zombie's head jerked up, her mouth bloody with part of Lou's sinewy muscles hanging out of it. Amelia hurled the scissors and they pierced the zombie's heart. Seeing that the zombie wasn't going to die, Amelia shrugged for the second time that day. Movies and books had always said the best way to kill the undead was to cause severe trauma to the brain. Her experiment with destroying the heart had failed, but at least she learned she could throw a pair of sharp scissors with decent accuracy.

Pulling her weapon out of her waistband, something she actually hated to do, she aimed and fired. A large, neat hole formed in the zombie's forehead. The back of its skull exploded, smearing its contents in every direction.

The high-heeled woman shrieked and rushed to unlock the door. She, along with her date and the third unknown male, exited.

"I can't believe you just killed her!" High Heels cried.

"Wasn't she with you?" Amelia asked to the third male.

He lowered his head sheepishly. "She was my girlfriend, but I was going to dump her after we left here. She could be a world-class bitch."

"Sloppy eater, too," Amelia quipped.

High Heels stood over the zombie and Lou, her mascara tears staining her skin as they ran down her face. "She was a human!"

"Not anymore, broad. Which reminds me…" Amelia's voice trailed off as she leaned over the counter.

"Did she just call me a 'broad?'" High Heels demanded, sniffling.

Amelia promptly shot Lou in the back of the head, his blood spraying onto High Heels.

"Ned! Ned! Get me out of here!" High Heels said with a squeal.

"Sorry if I ruined your date, Ned," Amelia said.

Ned smiled. "No way. I'm so going to get laid after I get her cleaned up."

Amelia turned to the third male. "I'm sorry for killing your soon to be ex-girlfriend."

"I suppose you did me a favor. Go ahead and get out of here. I'll take care of this."

Smiling at the memory, Amelia picked her favorite rock station and began cleaning her house. Her desk at work was what she preferred to call organized chaos, but her home was another story entirely. It might not be clean, but it always looked spotless. It made her feel calm after a long day at ZRT, whether it was an active day or not. Work wouldn't be so bad if it wasn't for the damn paperwork. She got it, though. File your version of what happened in the report so that, should anyone come and try to sue or do something else politically stupid, ZRT had the actual events covered. Reports were what had saved their asses from the Van Dutch family who slapped ZRT with a lawsuit after a particularly nasty encounter at their swanky mansion. What else did they expect would happen when they locked a bunch of infected in the attached guesthouse? Some people had woken up as zombies and charged the ones who were suspected of infection. By the time Team Mayfair had arrived, there were zombies with missing parts dragging themselves around. Amelia chuckled as she thought of the zombie missing one leg and how it had hopped after its potential victims. She found out later that had been Uncle Arthur, the patriarch of the Van Dutch family, that Rhys had finally put out of his misery. Uncle Arthur's will wasn't current considering his wife had died years prior, and everything was meant to go to her. The family was arguing about who received his fortune and blamed ZRT for his elimination. "We can't ask him questions with him dead!" they had cried. *News flash,* Amelia had thought then, *you couldn't have asked him anyway.*

Two hours later, Amelia was down to the last part of vacuuming. The music was turned up and she, per her personal tradition, was dancing with the machine as it sucked up dirt and debris from her floors. She badly but loudly belted out lyrics. Sometimes she wondered when her neighbors were going to complain about the noise.

A figure flashed in the corner of her eye and abruptly stopped. It was only her reflection in the full-length mirror of her bedroom, and she chastised herself for being jumpy. Continuing her vacuuming, she began to sing along to the next song and sway her hips to the beat. She wasn't a good dancer, either.

Another flash of movement and Amelia yanked off the headphones. She began to calculate how quickly it would take to get to the various weapons she had hidden throughout her home. There was a lot of open floor space between her and the nightstand containing the closest gun and she decided to do the next best thing: remove the extra-long attachment meant to reach high spaces.

The smell hit her fast and hard before the zombie actually entered the bedroom. She rushed it, holding out the attachment. Its jaws opened and she shoved the long piece of plastic into its mouth, satisfied as it promptly began to chomp. She reached into her nightstand and grabbed a .38 revolver. She aimed, then cursed. She had just cleaned this house! "You're going to have to work a little harder for your meal," she said.

Amelia darted past the zombie, ducking as it reached out to snatch her. It had already dropped the vacuum attachment. She ran down the stairs and quickly pulled the deadbolt and opened the door. She waited in the front yard and heard shambling behind her. She hardly had time to think as she spun around and swiftly sent two bullets into the new zombie's head. She turned back around to face her home, and the intruding zombie still hadn't come down. She swore again and hopped back onto her front porch, careful as she popped her head through the door. There it was, looking at her stupidly from the top of the stairs. "Well, come on, you dumb fuck!" It started to clamber down the stairs and she cringed at the dirt trail it was leaving behind and the one she noticed it left behind as it had gone upstairs initially.

The zombie finally found her outside and Amelia ended that one's life as well. Through a hole in the fence, she noticed yet another zombie working its way through the opening. She ran back into her home and grabbed the Kimber with spare magazines. She also took her radio and called to her teammates.

She closed her front door and waited until the third zombie was past the fence and shot it, too. She investigated the hole and found the missing board on the outside of the fence. It was her own fault for not figuring a zombie to be smart enough to remove a board to get into the property.

Suspicious that she had just encountered three zombies within a short period of time, Amelia began to hunt for others. There was a park nearby and she paused, listening and trying to catch the scent of decay. Inside the park was a swimming hole that everyone seemed to love on hot days. That was where she spotted two more zombies clumsily pulling themselves out of the water. She put them down and frowned as more seemed to follow.

"Amelia, where are you?" her radio squawked. It was Elisabeth.

"I'm at the park by the house. By the swimming hole. Bring a lot of guns."

"Don't you have an arsenal?" Rhys asked.

"I'll shoot you my damn self, Rhys."

"Ten-four," Rhys replied.

Dallas' truck barreled over the curb to the park and skidded slightly as it stopped nearby Amelia. Her team poured out of the vehicle, rifles out and ready.

Amelia pointed to the swimming hole where dozens of zombies were now accumulating. She looked at her team leader. "Shoot at any time, ma'am?"

"YES," ELISABETH RESPONDED. The bullets hit true to their targets as her team continuously fired. She inhaled deeply. Some of the undead were fresh, but some were very, very old. When they thinned down the herd, Elisabeth called ZRT.

"Bring me another team and some SCUBA equipment," she requested.

"Can't handle it on your own?" joked a young male voice.

"Who the fuck is this?" Elisabeth demanded.

The voice cleared its throat. "Ronnie Bacon. I'm the new dispatcher, ma'am. Sorry about that, ma'am. I'll get Team Aguilar over right away."

Overhearing their conversation, Rhys laughed. "You're going to fry his ass when you see him, aren't you?"

"I'll pretend I didn't hear that, son," Dallas said. "Shoot the damn zombies."

Another wave of zombies found its way into the park. "That's not your everyday swimming hole," Rhys said, his teeth gritted together as he fired shot after shot. He was almost as good as Amelia. Almost.

"Anyone got a grenade on them?" Dallas asked.

"No grenades!" Elisabeth shouted.

Dallas groaned. "You are out of your damn mind."

"If you shoot him for insubordination, I won't say anything," Amelia quipped.

A second vehicle joined them, this one driven by Luke Aguilar himself. He stepped out of the armored tank.

"You brought a tank?" Amelia asked.

"Don't be silly. I brought a tank on standard wheels. You said outbreak. We used the outbreak response vehicle." Luke patted the tank lovingly. "I've been wanting to break this baby out for a while now."

"Good to see you again, Luke," Elisabeth said. "Where's my SCUBA gear?" While the rest of his team joined her own in the eradication, she followed Luke to the side of the tank.

"Here's what you need." She ignored the wetsuit and slid the tank over her shoulders. It was smaller, but she wasn't even sure how far she was going yet. She kicked off her shoes and slid her feet in the flippers.

Luke nodded, threw the wetsuit back into the vehicle, and left Elisabeth to help his team. Only a few zombies were left now. Elisabeth began walking to the swimming hole when she felt a hand on her shoulder.

"You figured, too, that there must be a cave system down there," Rhys said.

"I did."

"What if you get stuck?"

"I appreciate your concern, but I won't get stuck."

Rhys frowned. He leaned forward and, his voice a whisper, asked, "Can you drown?"

"I don't know. I haven't tested that yet, but now isn't the time." Elisabeth slid her breathing mask over her face and flipped on her headlamp.

"I'll keep you updated on the radio," Rhys said.

Elisabeth jumped into the swimming hole. Immediately she realized this hole was deep, deeper than she had expected. She turned her body so that her feet were facing the surface of the water and she pushed herself toward the bottom. She quickly found what she was looking for: a dark opening illuminated in her headlamp.

Slowly, she kicked her feet and let the flippers do the work for her. She began to swim through a wide tunnel, pausing once in a while as it narrowed to check the size when she thought she and her tank might not fit. She really wasn't interested in finding out the answer to Rhys' question tonight.

The tunnel opened wide enough to fit a two-lane road inside and she felt herself let out a breath of air she hadn't realized she had been holding. A shape was in her way and she grabbed it by its foot. She wasn't going to let another zombie potentially harm her team. Elisabeth dragged the zombie until the tunnel opened into a large cavern. Still holding the zombie by its foot, she spotted a stalactite hanging from the ceiling. The zombie was writhing in her grasp, though not trying to bite her. Zombies thought Abnormals were also zombies and were never interested in their own kind.

She drew the undead to its feet and lifted it, smashing its head into the stalactite. It went limp instantly.

Elisabeth removed her breathing mask and her flippers. She took in her surroundings, which wasn't much other than what a person would expect to see in a large cavern. There was a light source nearby, and Elisabeth followed it to find the mouth of the cave. Searching around her, she noticed she was in an old, abandoned part of town. There was a small house with its windows missing, and Elisabeth hoped the poor people who had lived there had survived the attack. In her heart, she doubted it.

Feet bare, Elisabeth walked across the grass and toward the house. She entered through a broken door, already feeling her blood boil with anger. She found the kitchen and an old paring knife. It would have to do.

Walking into the living room, Elisabeth saw several other zombies. They weren't fully turned yet, but they would be soon enough. Dallas wasn't going to be happy with her, but she had no choice. She began systematically going from zombie to zombie—she couldn't call them people anymore—and stabbed them through their eyes with the small paring knife. Thankfully, there weren't many left for her to eliminate. She knew the horde that her team and Team Aguilar had encountered had originated here.

Back at the park, Elisabeth waved off the blanket Amelia offered. "Listen up," she said, her voice stern. "I found the source of the nest. It looks like someone has been storing the infected in a house about two miles from here in an uncleared part of town. They then lead them to the cave where they go into the water and pop out here."

"What do you mean, 'lead them?'" Luke asked.

"I mean someone is taking the zombies the short distance from the house to the cave and releases them."

"How in the hell can someone do that and not get eaten by the horde?"

"That's an excellent question," Elisabeth said. She caught her team eyeing her carefully. Team Aguilar didn't know she was an Abnormal. Elisabeth turned. "Dallas. You're going to get to use something a little stronger than a grenade."

"About damn time."

"ETHAN, WE'RE GOING to use the eco-bomb," Elisabeth stated. Despite her desire to return to the house and the cave, she had seen the weariness that her team tried to hide. Luke had promised to clear the park for them, though she knew that no more would be appearing through the swimming hole. She agreed and sent her team home for much-needed rest. Now she was on the phone and anxious for the leader of Division Tennessee to agree with her so that she and her team could do what needed to be done.

"No, you can just burn down the house," he replied briskly.

Elisabeth felt her muscles tense. Upper management could be a royal pain in the ass. "I don't want the local fire department out there for a controlled burn. More importantly, I want to search the house with my people before we get rid of it, and I don't want potential information to be seen by anyone else but ZRT employees."

Ethan Brown was struggling to breathe on the other end of the phone. He had contracted a yearly common cold as the weather transitioned to fall. Elisabeth had noticed she never got sick anymore, but she never really had before her bite. She wasn't sure if it was a symptom of being Abnormal or if her immune system was really that great of a defense against germs. Ethan either forgot to mute the phone as he loudly blew his nose or just simply didn't care that Elisabeth could hear him. When he finished, he asked, "How secluded are we talking here? Can people see the house?"

"No, they can't. It's in a part of town where no one lives and it's surrounded by the woods. The eco-bomb would destroy the house and any evidence it even existed. No fuss, no muss as they say. I don't want a burned skeleton left behind for some other crazy bastard to decide to use to rebuild on the foundation."

"You really think someone was taking infected people there and leading them off to the cave where they'd pop up on the other side?"

"Yes, I do. I think they were tranquilizing the people because they thought that the sleep would speed up the process. You and I both know it takes about a week for the infection to turn you with no symptoms, no warning. That last night is your last and you—"

Ethan cut her off. "You wake up a zombie. Yeah, I know the science lesson. The real question is this: who knew they were infected to begin with and took them to the house? Who guided them to the cave?"

Elisabeth stared at her shoes, her mind racing. "You know the answer to that as well as I do," she said bluntly.

"Fuck," he swore quietly.

"Ethan, how many other Abnormals are in ZRT?" Elisabeth asked tentatively.

"Classified."

"Oh, come off it, Ethan!" Elisabeth's patience was wavering.

"Can't you just sense them the way you sense the infected?"

Elisabeth paused before answering. "Are you being thick on purpose? Or are you just that stupid?"

"Watch your tone, Ms. Mayfair," Ethan snapped.

"I'm serious, *Mr. Brown*. I have never met another person like me. I have no idea if we all share the same effects from the bite. I don't know anything about them. I certainly can't tell you if I can sense them if I haven't been around one. Maybe I have been around one and just didn't notice because maybe they don't have the red eyes, but the bottom line is that I just don't know."

"You all have red eyes," Ethan said, his tone softening. "It's kind of freaky, really," he added.

"Then no, I haven't been around any other Abnormals," Elisabeth replied.

"I can tell you that when ZRT discovered your kind, they issued a statement claiming that the gases used to subdue the undead spread and had a permanent effect on people unfortunate enough to be nearby."

"That's not news. I remember that statement. I laughed when I heard it." Elisabeth could feel that she had wounded Ethan's pride. "I suppose ZRT had to think of something to explain to us so no one would be suspicious."

Ethan took a deep breath. Or as deeply as he could considering one nostril whistled noisily while the other clearly wasn't operating.

"Get what you can from the house. Use the eco-bomb. Seal off that cave, too."

"What about the swimming hole?" She already knew the answer, but sometimes it helped to stroke the ego of upper management to help them feel better about giving in to what she wanted.

"Block off the entrance to the tunnels at the bottom. There's no need to destroy something everyone else enjoys."

"Thank you, sir," Elisabeth said before terminating the connection. She walked out of her office and motioned for her team to meet her in the conference room. They filed in closely behind her and took their seats around the large table.

"Eco-bomb?" Dallas asked, his eyes hopeful.

"Yes. Rhys, I want you and Dallas planting the charges around the house and cave. Amelia, you're going to be with me while we search the house. I want to know who did this."

Amelia rubbed her eyes and nodded in agreement.

"Are we keeping you awake?" Rhys asked.

"Yeah, I'm a peach. I had to clean up the mess the zombie made before I could go to sleep. He ruined my vacuum attachment."

Dallas cleared his throat and looked at his team leader. "When do we leave?"

"Now."

AT THE ABANDONED house, Team Mayfair approached it cautiously. There were no more infected other than the dead ones whose bodies Elisabeth had left behind the previous night. She motioned for Rhys and Dallas to set the charges for the eco-bomb.

Inside the house, Amelia and Elisabeth began their search. The kitchen was empty save for a few utensils, including a large carving knife. Elisabeth held it up and thought of the paring knife she had used instead. She made a mental note to do a little more digging the next time she found herself in a similar situation.

Amelia led the way into what had been a home office. They discovered the home had belonged to a car salesman who had evidently been quite successful. "Who knew it paid so well to be such a smooth talker?" she said.

Elisabeth continued going through files when she felt Amelia stop. "Did you find something?"

"We're being a bit dense, aren't we? Who's going to keep their evil plan in the office? No, that's too obvious. Someone like that is going to go the more traditional route of crazy. We're going to find a wall full of photos in the basement or attic or a room at the end of the hall upstairs. Bonus points if they developed the photos themselves."

"You've got a good point," Elisabeth murmured.

"I know," Amelia said, winking. She left the office and Elisabeth followed her to a door in the living room. Even with the cooler temperatures, the bodies were already beginning to decompose. "What is a crazy lair in the basement, Alex?" Amelia asked as she turned the knob.

"Oh, we were looking for a coat closet. The answer was a coat closet," Amelia said, answering her own question. There was a single jacket hanging in the closet, and Amelia quickly rummaged through its pockets before closing the door and going upstairs.

Elisabeth smiled. She missed *Jeopardy*.

Upstairs, Amelia cried out, "Aha! What is the creepy room at the end of the hallway?"

The two women entered the last room and frowned. It had been the master bedroom. "No, this isn't right. There is no attic or basement. The other rooms were clear. Where is the crazy stuff?"

Elisabeth opened the door to reveal what had once been a decent-sized walk-in closet. "Here's your 'crazy stuff,' Amelia," she said.

Inside the closet was a single wingback chair. It had an old-fashioned floral pattern and barely a speck of dust on it. On the walls were sketches of several people, some with an X over their faces.

Amelia pointed at one of the sketches that had been crossed out in a thick marker. "That guy was in my house last night," she said, all traces of humor gone.

"Do you recognize anyone else?"

Amelia peered closer, her brown eyes narrowing in concentration. "Yes, though they were a little more decayed. They're crossed off, too."

"I recognize some of them as well." Elisabeth saw a drawing of the zombie whose head she had smashed in the cave. He, too, had a mark over his face. She couldn't tell if she knew any of the people whose faces bore no X, but collected the remaining sketches off the wall. Everyone would study them, and if they were infected, they needed to be eliminated immediately.

"I hate to be the one to bring this up, but this has to be another one like you. Those people downstairs hadn't turned yet when you killed them, yet the person who brought them here knew their fate."

"I know."

Amelia's eyes widened. "Did you tell Ethan Brown?"

"He knows, too. No, I can't sense another Abnormal. We do all have red eyes, though. Does that answer your questions?"

"For now. There's another problem, though. Again, I hate to ask this, but someone needs to, right?" Amelia was uncomfortable, her weight shifting from side to side as she contemplated the best way to ask her team leader such a direct question. Finally, she said, "Ma'am, can you die?"

Elisabeth raised a brow. "I don't know. I'm sure I can with a bullet to the brain just like anyone else."

"What about being wounded? Can you bleed to death like a human?"

"I don't know. I've never been hurt badly enough to risk losing that much blood." Elisabeth thought about Margo and her fears of experimentation. "I'm not interested in finding out, though."

"What I'm getting at is, if we go up against an Abnormal that is an enemy to us, we need to know how to kill your kind." Amelia exhaled loudly.

"If that happens, you're not to approach them. You're going to hang back and use those amazing shooting skills. You're going to leave the short-range combat to me." Elisabeth flashed a smile. "I appreciate your concern."

Amelia's eyes softened. "A lot of us lost loved ones. This team is like my family. It was too late for me to save most of my own, but I'll defend us until I die myself."

Elisabeth smiled warmly.

"We're done with the charges. Did you all find anything?" Rhys asked. He stepped past the women and let out an audible gasp when he saw the closet.

Dallas joined them and stood silently next to Rhys as he took in his surroundings. He pointed at the stack of papers Amelia held. "Those are people who haven't been crossed off yet?"

"Yes," she answered. She handed the sketches to Dallas and he flipped through the first few. He reached the fourth one and held it up. "No one noticed this one?" The team collectively shook their heads. "It's the mayor, folks. Seriously, y'all need to start getting involved in your local politics."

"The government is still fragile. The last thing we need is for people to lose the mayor, much less have him start eating the rest of the city council," Rhys said. "We need to wrap up here and get down to city hall."

"Speak for yourself." Dallas chuckled. "There's that one lady who has a stick shoved so far up her ass that she…" His voice trailed off when he caught Elisabeth watching him. "You're right, we need to finish up here."

The team exited the house and walked behind the company sport utility vehicle. "Is this far enough away?" Rhys asked. "I'm feeling lucky that today is the day Tammy will want to go out with me and I can't be sucked into nothingness."

"Keep dreaming," Amelia retorted.

"We'll be fine," Dallas said, unamused. Catching the nod from Elisabeth, he pressed the remote trigger. The air around the house began to swirl and create a miniature tornado. With each spin, the house shrank until it no longer existed. The entire process only took sixty seconds, and the only evidence left behind was the dirt on which the foundation had rested. The rest of the clearing had been untouched.

Dallas motioned for everyone to put on their ear protection. Soon, the team had neon pink foam—it was all that had been available—sticking out of their ears. He pulled out a second remote trigger and pressed it, subconsciously ducking as he did so. The cave imploded, the mouth collapsing in on itself.

When the dust settled, he and Rhys checked to make sure the entrance was sealed. Satisfied, they returned to the SUV and hopped inside to join Elisabeth and Amelia. "We need to block off the tunnels to the park," Elisabeth reminded them.

"What about the mayor?"

"If he's infected, he's not sleeping yet. It's not even lunch time. We have time." Elisabeth steered the vehicle away from the house and toward the park. It was two miles as the crow flies, but almost ten by car. Fifteen minutes later, they arrived at the park. With the temperatures dropping, she wasn't worried about being seen by civilians. For the second time in less than twelve hours, she was putting on her SCUBA gear, this time with the wetsuit.

Pulling her breathing mask over her face, she jumped into the swimming hole. The water was surprisingly comfortable, and she propelled herself farther down, charges in hand. She finally reached the bottom and floated into the tunnel. It was a little trickier adhering the explosives to the walls underneath water, but she did so as quickly as she could.

"You about done?" Dallas asked over the radio.

"On my way up now," she answered. She backed out of the tunnel and began to kick her way back up when she realized her tank was stuck. She must have turned at an odd angle as she'd tried to leave. Panic threatened to overcome her, and she kicked hard against the tunnel wall. It was a long way up and she needed the tank. She was wasting too much time. Inhaling as much oxygen as she could, she slipped out of the straps that held the tank in place.

Free from her confinement, she pushed herself upward. She could barely see the light above when she realized that she was almost out of air. Spots were forming in her vision and she involuntarily took a breath.

It was an odd sensation, the water filling her lungs. It chilled her to the core, but she felt relief. Her vision cleared and she reached the top, breaching the surface calmly. She crawled out of the swimming hole and began to cough violently. Water spewed out of her mouth and onto the grass. She inhaled and began to laugh uncontrollably.

"Rhys," she said when she found her voice. "I can't drown."

THREE

With her house so close by, Amelia had offered the use of her shower, which Elisabeth gladly accepted.

Rhys had been talking excitedly about the possibilities of other abilities Elisabeth might possess when she walked into the living room. She was pulling strands of her long, chestnut hair back into a French braid and a hush fell over the room. Rhys met her gaze, then continued his train of thought. "I wish we could do some more testing, preferably in a safe environment that we can control."

"I always thought the field was great for testing. See what you're really worth by being truly tested. Under pressure," Amelia said.

Rhys shot her a look, his brow furrowed. "Not all of us realized we weren't really afraid of people turning on each other to eat them like you did."

Elisabeth held up her hands. "That's enough. Let's not talk about turning your team leader into a lab rat just to satisfy your curiosity." She turned to Amelia. "While I respect your gusto, I'm not interested in field testing unless it's spontaneous. What if I had drowned?"

"Don't be ridiculous. I'm excellent at CPR," Amelia replied.

Half an hour later, the team was on their way downtown. Turning right into the parking lot, Rhys parked the SUV and twisted in his seat to look at the rest of the team. "How are we doing this?"

"You're going to wait here. I'll talk to the mayor on my own."

"In your armor?" Dallas asked.

"What better way to command his attention? Amelia, will you hand me those sketches, please?" Amelia leaned forward and handed them to her leader. Elisabeth tucked them underneath her arm. "Thanks," she said, opening the door.

The building had been turned into the town courthouse. It had been built in the 1910s shortly after the town of Pine Valley had been founded and was the original courthouse. It had been turned into miscellaneous offices over the years as a larger, more modern courthouse was erected. The construction workers of yesteryear built a more solid product because the new courthouse fell almost immediately. In protest of the slow response for the initial zombie outbreak, the community had burned it. Its charred remains were an eyesore and a taboo reminder of a society that had lost control of itself. It was too bad the eco-bomb had to remain a secret; Elisabeth would have destroyed the building already were she allowed.

While most mayoral offices weren't located in a courthouse, Pine Valley was a smaller town and they were still rebuilding. There were only so many people left, and fewer with the trade skills to bring the town back to its former glory. When the war ended, there were a lot of people who had only worked in an air-conditioned office and contractors or anyone with handy man knowledge was a commodity. Elisabeth hoped that as children grew, they were reminded that a valuable skill like plumbing was not one to be looked down upon in the future.

She entered the building and marveled at its old-fashioned tile. The architecture was beautiful, but today she could not enjoy the craftsmanship of long-dead workers. The security guard at the checkpoint began shaking his head as soon as he saw her and she flashed her ZRT identification.

"I still can't allow you through with those weapons, ma'am," he said, nervously removing his hat and running his hand through his light hair.

Elisabeth didn't need her guns to kill the mayor if he was infected, so she obliged. The security guard smiled with relief and put her belongings in a tray. She watched him put them into a locker behind him and slide a Master lock through the latch.

"These will be waiting for you," he said, then stepped back and let her through the second door.

She approached a desk where a petite, young woman sat. She was barely out of high school, but already had the presence of someone who had been alive for eighty years. *A zombie war will do that to a person,* Elisabeth thought.

"May I help you?" asked the woman, her tone cool and professional. She reminded Elisabeth of Tammy.

"Yes, I'd like to speak with Mayor Wilkins."

"May I ask who is visiting?"

"Elisabeth Mayfair with the Zombie Response Team."

The receptionist left her post and knocked gently on the door to the office behind her. Elisabeth heard the mayor shuffling papers and finally said, "Let her in." The receptionist beckoned with a long, spindly finger for Elisabeth to follow her.

"Please let me know if you need anything," she said before closing the door behind her.

Mayor Wilkins' office was very masculine. He had several deer antlers on the wall, a proud accomplishment from his younger days. He had a few hunting photographs, exquisitely framed, on his walls as well as a wet bar. She thought it was a bit stereotypical of a man's office in the 1960s, but she appreciated it. People needed to be reminded of a simpler time.

The mayor himself oozed confidence and politician. He was in his forties with neatly combed salt-and-pepper hair and bright green eyes that screamed intelligence. He stood and walked from behind his oversized desk to shake Elisabeth's hand. "Todd Wilkins," he said, his voice husky.

"Elisabeth Mayfair. It's a pleasure to meet you in person, sir," she replied.

The mayor pointed at the antlers. "I see you admire my work."

Elisabeth nodded. "I do."

"They fed a lot of families. I don't kill just for sport."

Elisabeth raised her brows, surprised. "I didn't think so, sir. Not many people in this area kill and leave behind the meat. Definitely not a politician who knows nothing can go to waste and wants to be re-elected."

Mayor Wilkins flashed a wide, easy grin. "You're not incorrect, Ms. Mayfair. Though I hope you don't think I do things just for show to stay in office."

"It doesn't matter what I think. I didn't vote in the local election, though I have a team member who would be very interested in that statement."

The mayor leaned forward, noticing Elisabeth's eyes. "You must have been dealing with the aftermath of those gases. I understand people in your position had to undergo invasive physicals to be cleared."

Elisabeth remained silent. That had all been a part of the statement ZRT had issued.

He cleared his throat uncomfortably. "Glad to know you're all right. Obviously. Anyway, Ms. Mayfair, what can I do for the ZRT today?" He sat on the edge of his desk, one leg dangling in a forced effort to seem casual. He motioned for Elisabeth to take one of his leather guest chairs.

She ignored him and pulled out the sketches instead. She pulled his off the top and handed it to him. "Do you know anyone specifically that would want to do you harm?"

The mayor balked at her directness. "Isn't that a question the police would ask?"

"Yes, but I'm asking and I need an answer."

He was quiet for a few moments as he thought about his reply. He handed back the sketch, shaking his head. "I can't think of anyone. Why would someone want to hurt me? Or any public official? We're picking up the pieces, getting stronger. No offense to you, Ms. Mayfair, but I'm hoping we won't need ZRT for much longer."

Elisabeth met Todd Wilkins' eyes, her gaze unflinching. "Because if the local government falls, people will panic all over again. We'll be where we were five years ago. We've come a long way in the three years since we eradicated most of the zombie population, but everything is still intensely fragile." She paused, thinking. The mayor watched her carefully. She gave him the rest of the sketches. "Do you recognize anyone else?"

He went through each one slowly, methodically, and placed two aside. When he had completed his search through the pile, he studied the two sketches again. "This looks like our judge, though he's been drawn a little heavier in this than he really is. This one looks like the man who will be running for governor."

"Will be? The election is next year."

"Yes, but one of the new laws we added is that no one can campaign for more than six months. The federal government decided that when they began to rebuild." He chuckled. "I guess even they were tired of campaigns that lasted for twelve to eighteen months."

Elisabeth scooped up the sketches and tucked them back under her arm. "I would suggest you be careful about where you go and, if you can, get someone to watch over you for a little while."

"How long is a 'little while?'"

"I'm not sure," Elisabeth admitted. "Until the threat is eliminated."

Mayor Wilkins slid off the desk and shook Elisabeth's hand once more. Still holding it, he said, "It was wonderful to meet you. I'm sure, with your cunning, you'll keep me safe. I hope to see you again soon."

Elisabeth felt herself flush. "Thank you." She left the mayor's office, thanked his receptionist, and spent her walk back to the checkpoint chastising herself for feeling like a school girl with a crush. She collected her weapons from the guard and waved goodbye over her shoulder as she walked down the steps and back to the parking lot.

Back inside the SUV, she relayed what had happened to her team.

"He's not infected?" Dallas asked. "Why is his picture on the wall? Why are any of their pictures on the wall?"

"I believe his elimination would cause a great panic within the community. The panic could spread. People will wonder if it was the work of an anarchist. They'll wonder if it will happen in other towns and cities. Whether people want to believe it or not, they need the government to guide them. We might not always agree with it, but there'd chaos without it."

"What about the judge and the man wanting to be the next governor?" Rhys asked.

"Scare tactic," Amelia answered quickly. "You remove a judge, someone in a high position like that, and people won't feel safe. If this governor wannabe disappeared, it would make people wanting to go into politics think twice. Why run for office when you might not even survive? We've all fought for survival for too long. Running for office shouldn't be a risk."

"Let's go back to the office. I need to talk to Ethan and see where we go from here."

Rhys put the vehicle in gear and turned onto the road. Amelia leaned forward in her seat, her head over Elisabeth's shoulder. "I heard Mayor Wilkins is super-hot," she whispered.

Elisabeth said nothing.

"I'll take that as a confirmation."

DALLAS ANDERSON WATCHED his team leader argue with the head of ZRT Division Tennessee. The blinds to her office were open and she was pacing back and forth, her hands on her hips, as she argued with the person barking at her on the other end of the phone. He knew she was in hot water for seeing the mayor before informing Ethan Brown of her findings first. He had wanted to suggest to her that they do that, but she had made it clear after the Libby Porter incident that his opinions weren't always appreciated. He understood why she wanted to see the mayor first and the positives outweighed the negatives, so he had kept his mouth shut.

He busily tapped away on his keyboard. He hated writing the daily reports as much as anyone else who worked for Zombie Response Team. He had to use the code words "green removal" in place of the eco-bomb because no one was supposed to know about that amazing piece of weaponry.

The printer was spitting out his finished work when he saw Rhys walk past his cubicle. He swore. He just wanted to give his reports to Tammy and wasn't interested in listening to the young man flirt with the office manager. The kid needed to know when to give up on a lost cause.

Oddly, Rhys was back sooner than expected, his face grim. Dallas had never seen him look serious. Rhys Gordon was carefree, happy. He had gone through hell with the rest of them and came out more appreciative of life. He considered any time not being chased by zombies a good day. This particular report had been difficult to write, as a person is forced to remember in agonizing detail the events that had taken place. He knew Rhys adored Elisabeth, looked up to her as a mother figure even though she roughly was the same age as he was. Dallas himself was the elder of the group, being in his late thirties. He was born in the wrong time and his prime should have been in the 1800s as a cowboy of the Wild West. His late wife had decided that for him when he took over the closet of their spare bedroom to house his collection of oversized belt buckles, bolos, cowboy boots, and Stetson hats. A smiled tugged at the corner of his mouth as he remembered her. She had been the most incredible woman he had ever known. He was grateful the cancer took her before those damn zombies had a chance.

Rhys will get over it, he decided. He gathered his reports, stapled them, and brought them to Tammy. Elisabeth was too busy to look over them and he figured she wouldn't mind Tammy's eyes being the first to see them.

She hardly noticed him as she looked over Rhys' account of the previous events. Dallas waited patiently and she finally looked up. "I'm so sorry about that," she said, taking them out of his hands. "Looks like the last twenty-four hours have been quite exciting."

"I didn't think you were allowed to read those."

Tammy laughed. "I'm the office manager. I follow the cliché that I know everything that goes on here. So, yes, I read every report that comes across my desk." She looked around, lowered her voice. "Officially, I check for grammatical mistakes. I can't send these in to headquarters in Nashville and have us look like a bunch of hicks over in East Tennessee."

"Do you find a lot of them?"

"Not as many as I thought I would. The educational system here isn't so bad. I hope they keep up the good work with the re-established schools."

Dallas tipped his hat. "Have a nice evening, Tammy."

"You, too," she murmured, her attention back on the paperwork.

Dallas stopped to say goodbye to Elisabeth, but she was still on the phone. She was obviously getting her way, though. Her expression had softened somewhat and she had stopped pacing. Instead, she was sitting in her chair, her feet propped up on top of the desk. That woman had a way with words.

He left through the breakroom and started down the long hallway. It led to the back entrance to the building, which he preferred because he liked getting to the office unnoticed in the mornings. He usually found members of Team Aguilar or Team Churchill leaving after a night shift. They all switched shifts every few weeks. He didn't mind the night shift. The nights typically held more action, which he preferred because it helped the time pass more quickly. Amusingly, it was mostly spooked phone calls more often than an actual problem.

It wasn't that he didn't enjoy his job, but he wanted to get back to normal, to being zombie-free. He wanted to do something completely unexpected, like open a pottery shop. Something he could enjoy creating and selling, and when he wasn't around, there would be no phone calls, no pottery emergencies. Until then, he did what he thought could help everyone the most, and that was kill the rest of the undead.

He pulled into his driveway and hopped out of his truck, reaching into the back of the cab to pull out the groceries he had picked up along the way.

"That you, Dallas?"

"Yeah, Dad," Dallas answered.

Hugh Anderson walked slowly into the kitchen, leaning heavily on his cane. He had lost a chunk of muscle from his thigh in a gruesome motorcycle accident when he had been in his late twenties. Dallas remembered the determination his father had shown as he learned to walk again and held a deep admiration for the older man. "What is that? Steak?" he asked.

"Rib eye, Dad. Thought we'd go the manly route of meat and potatoes."

"I've got the grill," Hugh said. He pulled the steaks out of the package and began to season them with salt, pepper, and chipotle. Seeing Dallas watching him, he said, "Gives it a little kick, don't you think?"

Dallas slapped his dad on his back. "You make the best steaks. You do whatever you need to do." He opened the bag of potatoes. "You want mashed, baked, julienne, or fries?"

"You don't mind doing mashed, do you?"

"Not at all." Dallas reached into the tin recipe box his wife, Rebecca, had kept. He had saved it specifically when he and his father fled their home. Cooking with her recipes made him feel closer to her. He started peeling the potatoes while he waited for the large pot of water to boil.

"You look like shit, Dallas," Hugh commented. He had returned from outside and was waiting for the grill to reach the right temperature.

"It's been a long day," he answered.

Hugh looked his son up and down. "It's been a long couple of days. You were barely home before you were back at it again. Is there a problem?"

"There was a horde that showed up by Amelia's house, but they're all gone now. We put the standby clean-up crew to work last night, that's for sure."

"Where'd they come from?"

Dallas hesitated. He didn't want to worry his father. "You know how it goes, Dad. We think we've got them all and then stuff like last night happens. I think they get caught somewhere and something happens, and then we're there to deal with them."

Hugh watched his son carefully. He wanted to probe more, but he knew his son had just lied to him and was already feeling guilty for it. Instead, he said nonchalantly, "That Amelia is a nice girl."

Dallas snorted. "She's all right, but a bit too much for me."

"Sometimes a man needs a woman to push him outside of his comfort zone."

"Knock it off, Dad. It's not going to happen. I had my perfect woman. I'm not interested in anyone else or even *being* with anyone else." He tossed the potatoes into the boiling water where they landed with a small splash.

"You'll change your mind," Hugh replied. He took the steaks outside where he remained for the next ten minutes as they cooked.

Dallas set the table for two and finished the mashed potatoes. He added the ingredients per Rebecca's handwritten instructions and tasted the white, fluffy concoction. "Perfect as always, honey," he said quietly.

He stepped outside and watched his dad remove the steaks from the grill. He reached to pick them up and his father raised his cane to block his arm. "Those need to rest."

"I know. But I'm helping you bring them inside." Hugh lowered his cane and Dallas wrapped his hand around the plate.

The two men ate in a comfortable silence, enjoying their meal.

When they finished, Dallas cleared the table and put the dishes into the sink. "You remember that rabbit you caught so we could eat one night?"

"I do. I also remember that's when you decided we let it go, and we had to fill up on blackberries."

"I couldn't go through with killing it."

"I respect that. But don't you ever bring blackberries into this house. I ate enough of those to last me a lifetime."

Dallas grinned. "Sure, Dad."

"I'm serious. My shit had never been so dark. Thought I was getting sick on top of all the craziness going on. No. More. Blackberries."

"All right, Dad. No more blackberries. What about blueberries?"

Hugh laughed. "Are those going to turn my shit dark, too?"

Dallas turned on the water and began to wash the dishes. "Dad, whatever happens between you and your excrement is for your eyes only."

Hugh lumbered over and picked up a towel. Drying a plate, he said, "I seem to recall a time when someone stole some packages off your doorstep."

"Dad, let's not talk about this anymore," Dallas pleaded, though the grin was still on his face.

"You didn't mind when I put my excrement in a box to use as bait and do you remember what happened?"

"The thieves stole the crap-filled box. After that, no one ever stole packages from my doorstep again." Dallas chortled.

"That's right," Hugh said matter-of-factly. He finished drying the glasses and put them back into the cabinet. He glimpsed at his son out of the corner of his eye as he closed the cabinet door and smiled to himself. His son's job was stressful but very important and Hugh understood that. If he could make his son laugh, then he knew that he was being helpful. In a world still struggling to get back on its feet, at least a father could still make his son smile.

THE DARK FIGURE stood a couple of yards from the Anderson household. It had listened closely while Dallas and Hugh discussed the horde and the destruction of the house. The figure wasn't upset about that; it would find another place to use. Pine Valley had never been large, but there were plenty of abandoned homes on farmland and it was common knowledge that the area was riddled with underground caves.

The figure wasn't even upset that its sketches had been found. It had anticipated their discovery and even threw them through a loophole with the bad sketch of the judge. It knew ZRT wasn't stupid, but they needed to believe they had found something tangible and real, not something that had been planted. The sketches that bore no X marks on them didn't belong to anyone; they were created. They served a purpose, though. With three belonging to real people who were still alive, the team would try unsuccessfully to identify the others.

Satisfied that Dallas wasn't going to divulge the sketches or Elisabeth's conversation with the mayor, it walked away slowly, leaving father and son in blissful ignorance of its presence.

ELISABETH PULLED THE Bluetooth out of her ear and smiled to herself. Ethan had been furious with her actions at first, but once she'd explained herself, he had calmed down significantly. He had even given her team free reign to investigate the issue and promised immediate assistance at her request. She was not to tell the other teams, which she did not agree with, but Ethan didn't want to have to explain why only Elisabeth could check for infection. "Until further evidence emerges, keep this between your team and me."

Tammy popped her head into Elisabeth's office.

"You're still here?" she asked.

"I had a lot of proofing to do before sending the reports out today, thanks to you," Tammy replied. "You're awfully lucky that you made it to the surface of that swimming hole after getting stuck with your breathing tank."

Elisabeth and her team had pointedly left out the part where she could breathe without the need of the tank. "Damn lucky," Elisabeth replied.

Tammy fished a handful of sticky notes out of her cardigan's pocket and handed them to Elisabeth. "Mayor Wilkins called several times. You were on the phone and I explained that you were busy."

"Thanks, Tammy." She looked through the notes. "Now go home," she instructed.

"You don't have to tell me twice."

Alone, she realized Tammy hadn't been exaggerating; he *had* called quite a few times. She picked up her phone and dialed his number, pleasantly surprised to discover it was his direct line when he answered.

"Ms. Mayfair! I see you finally were able to pry yourself away from your work to call me."

"Yes, I'm sorry about that."

Mayor Wilkins waited for Elisabeth to give an explanation along with her apology. When none followed, he continued, "I'm okay, so you don't have to worry about me. I'm a huge fan of the second amendment and, as you could see from my office, not a bad shot myself. I survived the war; I can make it with just a few of those zombies left."

It's more than just a few, Elisabeth thought.

"The reason I was calling was to, uh…" The mayor paused. Elisabeth could feel herself flush again and twirled her blinds so they were now shut.

"Yes?" she prompted.

"Ah, hell, I didn't survive the near apocalypse to turn coward now. I like you, Ms. Mayfair. *Elisabeth.* Would you like to have dinner with me tonight?"

Elisabeth suddenly felt exhausted. "I'm afraid I can't."

"Oh," the mayor replied, not bothering to hide his disappointment.

"I can go tomorrow."

She could almost feel Todd Wilkins brighten. "Yes, of course, it's already late as it is. I would love to pick you up at seven."

Elisabeth rattled off her address and the mayor hung up. For the second time in less than an hour, she smiled to herself. Because of the war, Elisabeth hadn't dated since high school.

No wonder she felt like a school girl.

"I NEED TO borrow something from you," Elisabeth said.

"Hello to you, too," Margo replied, opening the door wider to let in her sister.

"Hi, honey!" Ruth Mayfair called to her daughter.

"Hi, Mom," Elisabeth responded. Her mother sat in her oversized blue recliner, her hands working back and forth seamlessly as she knitted. There was an abundance of blankets around the house thanks to Ruth's favorite pastime. "This looks like it will be really pretty," she said, touching the end of the deep red fabric that lay bunched by her mother's feet. "That's really soft!"

"Thank you, Lizzy. This one's going to be my new bedspread, something cooler for the spring."

"I've told her that color isn't spring-appropriate," Margo said disapprovingly. Ruth stuck out her tongue playfully. "I know, Mom. You like the color and you don't care if it's in season or not."

"That's right!" Ruth said, her eyes gleeful. "Lizzy, honey, you really don't come by to visit often enough," she scolded.

"You could live here and she would think she doesn't see you enough. I know, I've seen her do it."

"Now, Margo, you're gone a lot for your job, too. Even more so lately it seems."

"We're almost back to where we used to be for the weekly newspaper. Just because it's released once a week doesn't mean I get to hang out here all day save for the day we go to print. I'm one of the reasons we have something for you to read." Margo worked as a reporter and editor for the small, local paper called *The Pine Valley Weekly*. It was often thin, but it was something the community looked forward to each Wednesday.

"Have you eaten yet?" Ruth had put down her knitting needles and was heading down the hall to the kitchen. She didn't wait for an answer. "You've probably just snacked all day. Let me whip up something for you."

Elisabeth knew better than to argue with her mother. She simply yelled down the hall, "Thanks!"

"What did you need to borrow?" Margo asked, turning Elisabeth's attention to her.

"I need something to wear for a date. You looted all of those old stores in the abandoned part of town a while back and I'd like to borrow one."

"It's not 'looting,' Lizzy. We were in hard times and I was tired of wearing the same filthy, blood-spattered clothes."

"I don't think Chanel and Dior are appropriate for an apocalypse."

Margo grinned. "Of course they're not, but if I was going to go out, I was going to look good doing it. Besides, we never reached apocalypse level, and now you're here asking for my pretty clothes." She led her sister down the hallway to her bedroom. They passed the kitchen along the way and her mother was busily whisking eggs. "Looks like it's going to be breakfast for dinner," she commented.

Elisabeth let out a low whistle when Margo opened her closet. It was crammed with different types of attire and the floor was crowded with boxes of shoes, their type facing outward for easy identification. "Is this all?" she asked sarcastically.

"Goodness, no. I've taken over another closet, too. There are some totes in the basement for the spring and summer months that I'll switch out next April."

"I suppose I should appreciate your need to be a clotheshorse." She began running her fingers over the different dresses. "Maybe just a nice top with my own jeans will do and some wedges."

"Wait, you said you needed something for a date. Who's taking you out?" Margo had her hands on her hips, her head tilted to the left quizzically.

"Todd Wilkins," Elisabeth answered quickly. She pulled out a lavender blouse and held it up to her chest. "How about this?" she asked, trying to change the subject.

"*Mayor* Todd Wilkins?" Margo practically shrieked. "You can't go out with him, Lizzy."

"Why, do you like him? You better tell me now so I can cancel tomorrow."

"No, I don't like him."

"Then what's your malfunction?" Elisabeth had replaced the lavender blouse and was looking at something in black.

Before she could pull the top off the rack, Margo blocked Elisabeth's hand with her own. "Not black. You always wear black with that drab armor."

"It's not drab," Elisabeth said defensively. "What's your problem with the mayor?"

"Yes, it is. I just don't think you should date a public figure, that's all. It could interfere with your job."

"Actually, my being around him more often will help ensure he doesn't get infected."

"You don't know that."

"Yes, I do," Elisabeth said mischievously.

Margo's eyes widened. "When did you find that out?" she demanded.

"I had locked you and Mom in that old storm cellar while I went to get supplies. Don't look at me like that. I thought the world was ending."

"You slut!" Margo laughed and lightly punched Elisabeth in the shoulder. "How do you know he didn't turn?"

"I saw him a week later. He was fine and heading to West Virginia."

"Would you have been able to kill him if he had?"

Elisabeth stared at her sister, her eyes narrowed.

"Of course you would have. You don't discriminate when it comes to the undead. Jokes aside, I love you dearly and I don't think seeing the mayor is a good idea. I don't trust him and I think this could be bad for you."

Elisabeth sighed. "I appreciate your concern, but I would like a distraction from work and the rest of the Reconstruction. Please, we have a mom and she can be concerned. I need my sister who has better taste than I do to help me pick out something that a very attractive man will find aesthetically pleasing on me."

"Noted," Margo replied, her tone serious. Brightening, she added, "Of course we'll find something that will look pretty on you." She winked. "After all, these look pretty on *me*."

ELISABETH WALKED QUIETLY back to her home while carrying the dress over her shoulder that Margo insisted she wear. Her mother and sister only lived roughly a mile from her, but she enjoyed the time to clear her head. Her mother had made her an omelet stuffed with mushrooms, cheddar cheese, and avocados. It definitely beat the days when Elisabeth had to hunt while Margo stayed behind to protect Ruth, though her mother was certainly no slouch when it came to self-defense. The truth was that Elisabeth preferred they remain safe while she took care of supplies because she knew she'd be all right on her own.

She began to walk into her neighborhood and the faint smell of decay invaded her nose. Comparing herself to a blood hound, she followed the scent and found herself standing in front of a gray house trimmed in white. She hung the dress on the lantern next to the doorbell, tested the door, and found it unlocked. She tried to open it and pushed harder when she felt resistance. The door swung open, and on the floor lay a woman with one arm draped over her chest and the other splayed out on the floor beside her. She looked fine except that her neck was at an odd angle and Elisabeth knew it had been broken. Breaking necks wasn't as easily done as the media had made it seem; someone had to have a lot of strength to do it.

In the living room, Elisabeth discovered a man lying on the couch, half of his skull missing and his arm still cradled in his sling. She shook her head; these were the people she had run into recently. They had been livid that she broke the man's arm, though Elisabeth still felt it was well-deserved.

On the kitchen wall hung a dull yellow phone and Elisabeth gingerly picked it up to dial the police. She explained the situation, swallowing hard after using the word "murder" in her description. The world had almost ended, been run over by zombies. Why would someone murder two innocent people who were clearly uninfected? The only thing the two had ever done wrong since the war ended was play a stupid prank on their friends. Maybe they would have found it funny had Elisabeth not misinterpreted the man's intentions.

Ten minutes later, a squad car, along with an unmarked vehicle, arrived. Elisabeth had been sitting on the stoop and stood to greet them. She shook their hands and the policemen went inside to see the scene for themselves. Elisabeth could hear them discussing the laziness of the coroner, who seemed unwilling to get out of bed to come to the crime scene. "He's gotten it easy writing 'Zombie Attack' next to the Cause of Death line on the certificates."

"Hank, don't be an ass. We aren't ready to start working murders again, either."

"Ma'am?" A man flashed his badge and Elisabeth saw he was Detective Brady. His hair was sandy-colored and closely cropped, but his goatee was surprisingly fluffy. "Can you tell me what happened here?"

Elisabeth recounted the recent events, carefully leaving out the part where she had been the one to break the man's arm. The last thing she needed was the police to be investigating her.

"How did you know that something was amiss?" he asked, his eyes piercing.

That's a great question, Elisabeth thought. She decided to be honest. "I was walking by and I could smell them."

The detective's brows furrowed. "Did you say you could *smell* them?"

Elisabeth tapped the side of her nose with her index finger. "I did. I've always had a really sensitive sense of smell. Came in handy when I had to hunt for food."

"It's not an effect of the gas that caused those eyes of yours?" His voice dripped with cynicism.

Elisabeth pretended to be offended. The man was clearly another conspiracy theorist who was closer to the truth than he'd ever know. "What part of 'always' don't you understand?"

"Had to ask, Ms. Mayfair." He scribbled notes onto a small pad of paper. "We'll be in touch if we need anything."

Elisabeth unhooked her dress from the lantern and began to leave.

"That dress belong to you?" Detective Brady asked.

"Nope," Elisabeth replied. It was her turn to be sarcastic and she felt the cop watching her as she sauntered down the street to her own front door.

FOUR

The next day, Elisabeth felt a growing knot in the pit of her stomach. She knew why it was there and felt childish for it. "Damn it, Elisabeth, you've battled several hordes of the undead and won. You're feeling anxious over a date? Get your head out of your ass," she said to herself.

"Am I interrupting?" Amelia asked.

Elisabeth glanced up, embarrassed.

Amelia spread her hands in front of her. "I can let you finish. I hate it when I'm having a conversation with myself and I lose my train of thought. Happens a lot around here."

Amelia wasn't teasing her team leader; she was being genuinely serious and that made Elisabeth smile.

"So you got a date, huh?" Amelia asked. "It's with that hot mayor, isn't it?" She planted her hands on Elisabeth's desk and leaned forward. "Where are you going? No, wait, when did he ask you out? Or did you ask him out? No, where is he taking you? Are you meeting there or is he picking you up? Are you being progressive and picking up him instead?" She paused. "Yeah, answer the one about how he asked you out first."

"I don't think you asked that one."

"Pretend I did." Amelia's eyes had a mischievous twinkle in them as she waited for Elisabeth to answer.

"He asked me after I returned his calls. He was fairly direct, actually. He's picking me up at my house. I don't know where we're going yet."

"Sounds fancy," Amelia said. "I hope you have a great time! I'd love to have a real date. For quite a while, I've just being throwing my V at any D that's willing. End of the world mentality, you know."

"You know the world didn't actually end?"

Amelia winked. "Role play."

"Isn't a bit too soon to role play that scenario?" Elisabeth put up her hands, palms outward. "No, don't answer that. What did you need before you started drilling me about the mayor?"

Amelia sat down in a generic guest chair across from Elisabeth. "I checked the system for missing persons and not one zombie from the horde we eliminated was a match. That's not to say they don't match what the next town over might have on their system. For some reason, they're still working on getting secure systems synced so that we can have access to everyone. Tech is saying about another four to five months until we get there."

"Really? That long? We've gotten so far already and we can't access each other's missing person files?"

Amelia circled her finger around her ear. "Crazy, right? It is what it is, though. Would Ethan approve me going to an adjacent town to check it out?"

Elisabeth shook her head. "No, he won't. The ZRT won't allow any one team member to travel on her own. We can only go in groups on official business and this is sort of under the rug at the moment."

"You want to burn the bodies, then?"

Elisabeth ran her fingers through her hair. "Get photos of them. When they get through the oven, be sure to put each one in an urn and don't dump the ashes in the communal bins. Get Rhys to help you separate them from what Team Aguilar and Team Churchill bring in so Chick with cleanup doesn't mix them."

"We've got plenty of coffee cans."

"Put the ones that are further along in decomposition, the ones that are barely recognizable, in the coffee cans."

"Will do, ma'am. Have fun tonight." Amelia stood up to leave and winked once more. As she left the office, Rhys walked past her. She grabbed his arm. "Whoa, Rhys. We've got to go put some dead people in coffee cans."

"Never a dull moment around here," he joked.

Elisabeth glanced at the clock and decided to leave early. She checked in with Dallas to make sure that he didn't need anything else from her. Feeling guilty, she left through the back door.

At home, she felt giddy as she showered off the day and curled her hair. It had been ages since she'd actually done anything with her hair other than leave it straight or sweep it up into a ponytail. Margo was the one who loved fashion, loved applying layers of makeup, and making sure that she didn't leave the house with a strand out of place, even if it was meant to look unkempt. She wasn't a whiner, though. With the war going on, she was determined to make the best of it. She had easily shed her "girly girl" persona and became a warrior and a survivor.

Elisabeth slid into the dress her sister loaned her, though honestly she doubted Margo would ever want it returned. It was a long-sleeved black chemise with a splattering of small flowers on it. Her sister had even given her a pair of suede dove-gray over-the-knee boots to go with it and Elisabeth felt downright sexy. Margo had called the color of the shoes "fungi" and Elisabeth had told her that was a disgusting name for a color.

She checked herself in the mirror once more as her doorbell rang. Todd Wilkins was wearing a dark suit. He tried unsuccessfully to be discreet as he looked over Elisabeth. "You look very nice," he said finally.

Elisabeth smiled. "As do you," she replied.

He smoothed his suit jacket. "This old thing? Thanks, ma'am."

Elisabeth stopped moving. "Okay, I'm going to be direct and tell you that if you ever call me 'ma'am' again, I will disembowel you. I get called that enough during the day."

"That's a bit extreme, isn't it?"

"I need to impress upon you how serious I am."

"Duly noted, Ms. Mayfair."

"I think we can be on a first name basis, Todd."

Todd laughed nervously. "I must admit it's been so long since I've been out with a lady that I have almost forgotten the etiquette." He watched Elisabeth check her purse for her keys. "You're not going to carry anything else with you?"

Son of a bitch, Elisabeth thought. "Of course. I suppose I forgot the rules of going out myself, though carrying should be considered a new rule." Todd sat down on her sage green couch while she went to her gun locker, grabbed a .22, and slid it into her pocketbook. It was a wimpy gun in her opinion, but the mayor didn't need to know about her special abilities. She stepped into her living room. "All set now," she said.

THERE WEREN'T MANY restaurant choices in town, but the people didn't mind. They were just happy to have restaurants again. Todd had chosen *Romeo's*, claiming they couldn't go wrong with Italian food.

They were seated in a small, intimate table near the back of the restaurant and served quickly.

"What made you decide to run for mayor?" Elisabeth asked, taking a sip of her house red win.

"I wanted to help the community. Honestly, I'm not someone who is good at working with my hands. I was raised in a house of fellow politicians. This was the best way I knew how to contribute."

Margo had taught Elisabeth that the best way to get more information out of people was to simply remain silent. She was right.

"I didn't know what else to do," he added nervously. "How did you get into ZRT, much less get to be their leader? Aren't you, excuse me for saying, a bit young?"

"I'm older than I look," Elisabeth said, pretending to be defensive. "Nonetheless, I do appreciate subtle compliments. Thank you."

She flashed a smile. More seriously, she told him, "I stumbled upon it, actually. My family and I were moving. We moved a lot during the war because we felt that was the best way to stay alive. One day I was at a pharmacy gathering various medicines when I heard shooting. I ran outside and saw a group of men in black shooting at an even larger group of zombies. Another man who, I'll never forget, was wearing khakis and a mint button-up shirt came out of seemingly nowhere and joined the men. I stashed the medicine back in the pharmacy and began shooting, too. We destroyed them all and that's when Ethan Brown noticed me. I couldn't believe this small man in his silly mint shirt was in charge. He offered me a job and my family and I came here to Pine Valley."

The truth was that Elisabeth, after having stashed the medicine, ran around the block until she was behind the horde and began to shoot. When she had run out of bullets, she started punching through the backs of the zombies' skulls. When she had thinned the horde to the point where she feared detection, she ran around to where she was behind the men. One of them threw her a gun and she caught it, firing it immediately. Ethan had turned to thank her when he suddenly stopped, startled. He had gestured for her to move somewhere more private and told her he knew exactly what she was, and no, she needn't worry. He knew how to put someone with her condition to good use and Elisabeth had obliged happily.

"Just like that, he offered you to part of ZRT? No other interview process?" Todd's voice was heavy with disbelief.

"We have more extensive screening now. Back then, you just needed to know how to shoot a gun and not be afraid to die. Those two are still the most important traits we look for, by the way."

"You're not afraid to die?" Todd asked, his tone softening.

"I worry about my family, about other people. There isn't enough room to worry about myself." Elisabeth loathed lying, didn't tolerate liars normally, but she couldn't tell the mayor the truth. She wasn't afraid for herself because there was not a reason to, not since the bite.

"We each do something good in our own way. Yours is quite more action-packed than mine. I can't imagine the things you see each day."

"You're the mayor. Shouldn't you be more involved?" Elisabeth asked.

"This Ethan Brown of yours is a slippery fellow. He gives me enough information to keep me pacified, though I would like to know more." Todd reached across the table and placed his hand over Elisabeth's.

Elisabeth withdrew her hand. Her expression darkened. "If that's why you asked me out, then you're out of luck. I'm a fiercely loyal person, Todd. That might not be the case in politics, but in my line of work, if you don't have loyalty, you don't have anything."

Todd raised his hands. "I'm sorry, that was the wrong moment to touch you. I'm such an idiot. I wouldn't ask you to betray your employer's trust. I'm sorry."

Several moments passed in silence as Elisabeth looked him over, deciding if she should leave. Finally, she said, "Apology accepted. You are an idiot, but you'll get better at this."

"Does that mean you'd be willing to go on a second date?" he asked, hopeful.

"It does." Elisabeth smiled and he leaned across the table, his hand outstretched to tenderly tuck her hair behind her ear.

Instead, the server returned with their meals and placed Elisabeth's eggplant parmesan in front of her. Todd pulled back, the moment gone, and let the server put his spaghetti in front him.

"Thank God for next times," he said underneath his breath.

THEY SPENT THE rest of the evening enjoying light conversation, purposefully avoiding any serious topics. Elisabeth touched her lips absently, still feeling the warmth of his mouth on hers. Todd had been hesitant as he leaned forward and she met him halfway. He thanked her for a good night and promised to call the next day.

She stepped out of her dress and threw it into her hamper. Margo would have a fit if she knew Elisabeth was going to hand-wash it instead of taking it to the dry cleaners, but what her sister didn't know wouldn't hurt her. She slipped a T-shirt over her head and pulled on green pajama shorts. After brushing her teeth and washing her face, she crawled into bed, loving the warmth of the heavy beige comforter she had found on one of her supply hunts. Her family had wanted her to get rid of it because it reminded them of the nights they spent underneath it, along with several other blankets, trying to stay warm. Elisabeth couldn't bear to part with it; it reminded her of something that helped save her life, albeit in a small way.

Elisabeth fell asleep peacefully, her slumber dreamless.

THE FIGURE WATCHED Mayor Todd Wilkins leave Elisabeth Mayfair. It needed to infect him, but with Elisabeth watching him like a hawk until he pulled out of her driveway, there was no opportunity.

The figure was torn. It wanted Elisabeth to be happy, and harming the mayor would contradict that plan. Unfortunately, his elimination truly was for the greater good.

Hopefully, Elisabeth would realize that.

JASON WILSON HATED scavenging. His family had set up a booth at the local flea market and sold mostly junk, though people seemed to love it. He went all over the region picking through old barns, houses, basically any dwelling that looked promising. They seemed to do well with old, metal signs and 1950s-style furniture. Old crap like that seemed to help their particular clientele remember a better time prewar. He wished they would just get over it already. A virus broke out and spread fast because there were no symptoms for seven days. By the time some bureaucrat got the bright idea to screen everyone and make people carry a blood book, it was too late and the world crashed. Well, almost crashed. The government in the United States never truly fell. He didn't know about the rest of the world and didn't care. He wasn't leaving the country and never planned on it. He hated his job, but it supported his family and he was lucky they all survived. He knew a great many hadn't had such good fortune.

His father had a rule that all scavenging be done in pairs because you just never knew with the places outside the safe zones. He and his cousin, Jeremiah, followed his father's wishes at first. Now they left in a pair and split as soon as they were out of sight. A person could cover more ground alone and he wasn't really afraid of anything anyway. He'd made it through the war when thousands of zombies were a constant threat. How bad was it going to be with so few left behind? He could take them then and he could take them now. His uncle provided them with the bullets and he had never failed. He wasn't about to let anyone down now.

Jason rode a bicycle with a wagon attached at the back. The truck was saved for the big stuff they found because the family only had one vehicle. He was riding down an old gravel road that had more weeds growing through it than actual pebbles. The wagon clanked loudly behind him, but Jason didn't mind. It was a beautiful day with blue skies and weather cool enough that he didn't sweat as he peddled for hours searching for trinkets.

He approached a gate across a cattle guard and laughed softly at the *No Trespassing* sign. He opened the gate and left it that way; no sense in closing it behind him. A mile later, he came upon an old, crumbling white house that had once seen a lot of hardworking farmers. If this piece of land had been inside the safe zone, he would have suggested that his family commandeer it and start farming themselves. They grew a few vegetables, but it was to supplement their own diets. With this kind of land, they could earn enough money to get rid of the booth and he could stop spending countless hours doing something he so thoroughly loathed. *Maybe one day, if they can clear it all out in a year or two*, he thought hopefully.

Jason got off his bike and put the kickstand in place. The white house rested on top of a hill, and farther down was a small barn. Removing his rifle from the sling across his back, he checked the property for any undead. Next, he methodically searched the house and barn before he began tossing in items he found interesting into a pile by the front door. He'd have to talk his dad into letting him bring down the truck and Jeremiah would actually have to join him. The house had a lot of antiques, including an old pie cabinet he knew his mother would want for herself.

He took several trips between the house and the wagon, filling it up almost completely. He quickly relocated his bike to the front of the barn and began to pick up a few pieces that he had seen on his initial walk-through. Customers liked old wood, and used it for decoration and shelves. He threw some old slats on top of the wagon and, with it being at full capacity, strapped down the contents.

Jason straddled his bike, ready to leave, when he noticed a small outbuilding almost hidden between the valleys of the small hills that dotted the land. He eyed his wagon and decided he could squeeze in a few other items if necessary.

As he approached the building, he noticed immediately that were no windows except for one too high to see through unless he had a ladder. Unfortunately, it had a locked chain around its doors that refused to budge when he pulled as hard as he could. He wasn't about to come this far and not scour every inch that was available. Nearby, he found a few old hay bales and kicked them to check for snakes before hauling them one at a time underneath the window. The hay was itchy as it scratched his skin, but he paid it no attention. Creating a staircase, he climbed the bales and looked through the window. Cupping his hands around his face to see more clearly, he saw nothing inside but a few lumpy sheets and—Jason Wilson did a double-take—a door!

It looked like a trap door on the floor, complete with ring handle. It had been used recently; there was not any dust covering it. Jason squinted and realized that there were footprints around the door. What in the hell was happening here?

Suddenly, one of the sheets began to *move*. It raised upward, then fell away. Jason watched, unable to tear away his eyes as the sheet revealed a person. It was a middle-aged man and he was looking around the building in bewilderment. He looked upward and locked eyes with Jason. With inhuman speed, he lurched forward, on his feet and walking toward the window. His foot snapped backward, caught by a coil of rope on the floor. The harder the man tugged, the tighter the rope became around his ankle. Stuck, he began to moan.

"Holy shit!" cried Jason, nearly stumbling backward down the makeshift staircase. He didn't have enough bullets for what was in the outbuilding and leaped off the hay bales. He ran to his bike, his heart thudding in his chest as he heard the chains around the door begin to rattle. He peddled as quickly as he could, never slowing until he reached the safe zone. There were no guards for these areas anymore; they had gotten rid of them months ago. It had been decided if that you're foolhardy enough to leave, why should anyone try and stop you?

Heart still pounding, he finally arrived at Zombie Response Team. Ignoring the kickstand, he jumped off the bike and it crashed to its side. He didn't have time to notice; he was already inside the building.

"I JUST SAW a bunch of zombies! You have to get rid of them!" cried a young man, his skin shining with sweat and his dark hair disheveled.

"Calm down. Take a deep breath," Tammy Goodwin said, her voice even. She would have made an excellent 911 operator.

The man slammed his hands down on the top of her desk. "I don't want to take a 'deep breath!' I just saw a shit ton of zombies and I couldn't take them out myself. You guys need to do it!"

Hearing a loud bang in front of the office, Rhys trotted up to check on Tammy. He found a young man in his late teens in a panic, his hands clenched into fists. "What's your name? What's the problem?" he asked. He displayed no urgency, no sense of concern. He didn't want to further upset the man.

"I'm Jason Wilson," he answered. He wiped his hands on his jeans and held out one to shake.

Grasping his hand firmly, Rhys introduced himself and waited for the man to continue.

"I was out at a farm. I think it was the old Bentley farm, but I was only there once as a kid and some of those places all start to look the same after a while. There's an old outbuilding there and it's chock-full of zombies. You need to get out there and kill them."

Rhys didn't bother asking what he was doing outside of the safe zone. "How many do you estimate are there?"

Jason clasped his hands together on the back of his head. "I don't know. Dozens!"

"Okay, okay," Rhys said soothingly. "You did well, Jason."

"Thank you, sir," Jason replied. He laughed nervously. "I guess I did my part and I can leave now. Right?"

"We're going to need you to take us back out to the farm, I'm afraid." Rhys felt guilty for asking; the young man was obviously shaken.

Jason paled.

"You'll be fine. I promise."

Fifteen minutes later, the team had donned their armor and Jason Wilson had parked his bike and the wagon in their office. They piled into the SUV, Jason between Dallas and Amelia in the back seat.

"I'm a scavenger," he explained. "My family has a booth at the flea market and we sell stuff from before the war. We don't have a choice and have to go to the areas that haven't been cleared. I can take care of myself, but I don't expect to run into that many biters anymore, so I don't carry that much ammo. It's hard enough lugging around the wagon sometimes when it's loaded."

Amelia patted his knee reassuringly. "You're not in trouble. I know which booth you're talking about and you all have a lot of neat things. Might be better off going picking in pairs, though."

Jason hung his head. "We're supposed to. Please don't tell my father."

"Your dad doesn't have to know anything. I had plenty of secrets from my parents when I was your age."

"Like what?" he asked.

Dallas threw a sharp look at Amelia.

She cleared her throat. "Stupid teenager stuff." She flashed a smile at Dallas. "Sneaking out to see boys, mostly."

"Amelia," Dallas warned.

"Oh, shut up. It wasn't like that. We had a shooting club. I was the best. Naturally. I took them for a lot of money because they always bet against me. It got to the point where we had genuine bookies that would trick newcomers to betting against me and everyone was making some extra cash. Great gig."

"Why couldn't you just be a pool shark like a normal person?" Dallas asked.

Rhys whistled low. "The answer is in your question. When have we known our Amelia to do something normal?"

Elisabeth said nothing. She knew that was an unspoken sore subject for Amelia, though she would never admit it to the men.

"Are we close?" Rhys asked.

"Make a left turn up here," Jason instructed.

"I don't see a road."

"It's there," Jason reassured him. "See that gate? Wait, it's closed. I left it open."

"Are you sure?" Elisabeth asked.

"I'm positive. I hauled ass out of there. I wasn't going to stop to close a dumb gate to some abandoned house."

Rhys brought the vehicle to a crawl and crested the last hill. The house and barn were in plain sight and looked the same way they had when Jason left originally. "Clear this first, ma'am?" he asked.

Elisabeth nodded. She ordered Amelia to wait with Jason while she and the rest of her team searched the property. Finding nothing of interest, they drove to the outbuilding. It was hard to see from the house because of the layout of the land and Elisabeth was surprised that Jason even noticed it.

Jason went to open the back door and Elisabeth stopped him. "Give me a gun and let me help. I feel badly enough that I left this problem out here."

"Not a chance. You stay here and lock the doors." When Elisabeth gave orders, no one argued with her. She knew she had intimidated the poor young man, but she wanted to know he was safely locked away in case something went awry.

"Clever kid," Dallas said, pointing at the hay bales. He took point and climbed upward, looking through the window when he reached the top. "Oh, yeah. There are zombies in there. We might be better off with something more powerful." He looked hopefully at Elisabeth.

"You got to blow up things a few days ago."

"I know. I like that kind of thing."

Elisabeth hid a grin and ducked behind the side of the building where the doors were located. "We need to check out where that door leads. Amelia, get up there with Dallas and break the window. Start shooting. Rhys, you're going to be here with me. I'm going to open the door and you shoot whatever comes out. Everyone understand?"

"Zombies bad. Shoot guns," Rhys replied.

Making sure Jason couldn't see her from the SUV, she yanked the chain and it broke easily. She unthreaded it from the handles and swung the doors open as wide as they could go. She quickly counted thirty-seven zombies before she backed away and began to fire her weapon. They were falling quickly as her team picked them off one by one.

Dallas managed to shoot one through the head and the bullet continued, lodging in the head of another zombie that had been standing behind it.

"Damn, that was great!" Amelia cheered. Seeing one escape the barn and head in her direction, she quickly put it out of its misery. "Hey, Rhys, why don't you get better and not let them slip past you?" she chided.

"Sorry," Rhys said, gritting his teeth as he fired.

"I don't think that was sincere," Amelia replied, shooting through the gap between the door and the building and bringing down another undead.

"That woman is going to give me a Napoleon complex," Rhys complained.

Dallas put down the last zombie and Elisabeth entered the building to do a final check. She saw one more hidden beneath a sheet and shot it. It hadn't even had a chance to turn completely, but it had been close. She gestured for Amelia to return to the vehicle to stay with Jason while she peered at the door curiously.

"This probably covers the cistern for the well," Dallas said. "Don't normally see these things covered with a building, but I suppose to each his own. Not my farm, not my cows."

"Step back, please," she said as she lifted the door and slid it to the side. She reached into her cargo pocket, removed her flashlight, and used it to look into the compartment. It had been a cistern, but now there was a hole in the bottom. "Another goddamn tunnel," she cursed.

"At least this one isn't under water," Rhys said.

"Keep your eyes open," she said and dropped down in the compartment. As she got onto her knees and began to crawl, she heard Rhys chuckle. "Something funny?" she asked harshly into her throat mic.

"Not at all. Just glad you're the special one here, that's all," he answered.

The tunnel was the width of two people and just as tall. It was old and Elisabeth wondered if maybe it had been used in the Underground Railroad. Thinking of its possible rich history occupied her mind as her knees banged painfully against the floor. She finally came to a small opening, the air thick and damp. She was in another cave, though this one had no light, meaning no entrance nearby. She shined her flashlight around the walls until she found another opening, this time one high enough that she could walk comfortably through and give her knees a rest. She made a mental note to add knee pads to her gear bag in case she found herself in another tunnel.

The passageway was short, and she walked into a larger cavern. There was equipment on one side and Elisabeth realized this hadn't been for the Underground Railroad. Someone used to make moonshine and the tunnel was the delivery system, the outbuilding used as storage. *People will get creative when you take away their booze*, she thought.

With the equipment in sight, Elisabeth knew there had to be an entrance fairly close. She passed through two more passageways when she began to see natural light and turned off her flashlight. There were crude stairs carved into the floor and she took them, being careful not to fall on the slippery floor. The ceiling lowered suddenly and she had to hunch over to fit. Brush and debris covered the entrance and she pushed them back to exit.

There was nothing.

She was standing by the side of a large hill looking over a meadow. It was fairly big and melted unevenly back into the surrounding forest. Some of the grass had been flattened, but she couldn't determine if they were human footprints or caused by an animal.

She walked into the woods, her ears straining to hear anything unusual. They were very dense and she could find no other signs that might indicate a human had been out there.

A twig snapped and Elisabeth whirled around and found herself face to face with a black bear. Its mouth was wide open, its breath putrid. She gingerly stepped back and the bear reached out, swiping its paw and barely missing her.

She ran as quickly as she could until she was back at the meadow. She jumped behind a tree and slammed her body against it. The tree crashed to the ground, blocking the bear. It was only a temporary fix and the bear would soon be able to figure out that it could either go around or climb over the tree. Not wanting to see its choice, Elisabeth rushed through the cave opening, the branches scraping her face as she passed.

She flicked on her flashlight and scurried through the passageways until she reached the smaller tunnel that had led her there. Knees bruising, she crawled as quickly as she could until she reached the familiar opening and practically leaped out. She slid the lid back on and stepped back. Her face stung as her sweat mingled with the blood in the cuts on her cheeks. A bead of sweat threatened to drop into her eyes and Rhys reached automatically to wipe it away. She caught his arm. "Don't touch my blood. Regular body fluids aren't infectious, but I don't know about the blood."

Rhys mumbled an apology, embarrassed.

"Did a zombie attack *you*?" Dallas asked.

"No, it was a bear."

Dallas' eyes widened. "You got attacked by a bear?" He was incredulous.

"They're hungry, too."

"Are we going to be handing out bear meat to the local butcher?"

"No, Rhys. I left him alive."

"Holy shit, you're a bad ass!" Rhys exclaimed.

Elisabeth looked at him warily.

"Ma'am," Rhys added.

Dallas was shaking his head. "Did you find anything down there?"

Elisabeth explained her discovery.

"Moonshine. Really?" Rhys said, his brows raised.

"Don't get excited. There was none and that equipment is so old that I'd be surprised if it still worked."

"What do you think this is?" Dallas was looking at her thoughtfully and she knew he had reached the same conclusion.

"I think we destroyed someone's zombie lair, for lack of a better term. They moved on to this spot."

Dallas' eyes lit up.

Before he could ask, Elisabeth said, "Yes. Go get your stuff."

He ran back to the car, and reached into his gear. "Rhys!" he yelled. "Help me carry these!"

"You look like a kid on Christmas morning," Amelia said.

The team, including Jason, was sitting in the SUV Elisabeth had moved farther away from the building. Without preamble, Dallas clicked the remote trigger and they watched the outbuilding explode. When the debris settled, Dallas checked to make sure the tunnel had been blocked. "No one is getting in that tunnel except for someone like you," he murmured to Elisabeth when he returned.

"Someone like her?" Jason asked, leaning forward.

"No one likes it when you're nosy." Amelia put her arm across his chest and pushed him back against the seat. "Don't be rude."

FIVE

"I don't have to ask you to leave out the bear attack in your report," Elisabeth said.

"We weren't there. How would we possibly be able to report it?" Rhys winked at her and walked back to his cubicle.

Elisabeth shut her office door behind her. She pinched the bridge of her nose and slumped in her chair. She ached everywhere, especially her knees. Her left shoulder was screaming from where she had knocked over the tree. She was grateful for the super strength the bite had given her, but she was greedy in that she wished it came with no consequences like pain from using her abilities. She knew she could have handled the black bear, but she also knew she would have sustained damage as well. She didn't want to be stuck at home nursing her injuries and leave her team, so she had run instead.

She stared at the phone for several moments. She knew she would have to call Ethan and tell him everything. He was going to want to know why she found another building filled with zombies and yet another cave attached. He would ask her if the team recognized any of them, she would say no, and he would ask her where in hell all of the zombies were coming from. She wouldn't have an answer for that either.

Stop being a pussy. He's just your boss. She picked up the phone.

RHYS GORDON WATCHED Elisabeth hang up the phone. She looked tired and worn down. He didn't envy her position. He knew the head of ZRT Division Tennessee could be difficult and he wished that they had the answers to their current situation.

They were lucky that Jason Wilson had found the nest. He had collected his bike when they returned and Rhys warned him privately about the dangers of his family business.

"I know, but this is what we do," he had said quietly. Rhys made him promise to never venture out unless he had a partner.

"I mean it, Jason. It's still dangerous out there."

"Yes, sir," Jason had promised.

Rhys tapped out the last of his report, printed it, and brought it to Tammy.

She held up one finger. "Don't even start."

He flashed her his most charming grin. "I wasn't going to."

"Yes, you were. Just hand those over," she said, her hand outstretched. She took the reports and noticed a bright yellow sticky note on top. She scanned it, looked around her, and whispered, "That's fine." She tore the note into tiny pieces, crumpled them, and threw them into her trash can. She grabbed a few more sticky notes, balled them up, and tossed them into the garbage for good measure. "Don't hand me notes again," she said under her breath.

"As you wish," Rhys said.

"And don't quote *Princess Bride* either," she added.

LATER THAT NIGHT, Rhys poured spaghetti into a colander, draining the water. He picked it up and shook it a couple of times to ensure that all of the excess water was gone, then put it back into the pot. He checked the temperature of the tomato sauce and began to set the table.

He had returned to the kitchen to plate the spaghetti when he heard a key turn in the lock. He continued loading the pasta onto the plates and pouring sauce over it, topping off each dish with a sprinkle of parmesan. He put down the plates and returned to the fridge. "Would you like something to drink?" he asked.

Tammy Goodwin replied, "Do you have any tea?"

"Iced or hot?"

"Iced."

Rhys came out of the kitchen, a beverage in each hand. Tammy waited for him to set them down before circling her arms around his waist. He returned the embrace, running his fingers through her short hair. "How was your day, honey?"

"It was fine. There's this guy at work who keeps hitting on me, though." She nuzzled her nose against his before sitting down and putting her napkin on her lap.

"Is there, now? Do I need to kick his ass?" Rhys asked.

"No need. I can handle it." Her face broke out into a smile. "How much longer are we going to keep this up and not tell anyone else we're dating?"

Rhys twirled the pasta around the tins of his fork. "I kind of like it being a secret. You should hear the way I get teased and told to just 'give up.' If they only knew." He took a bite of the spaghetti. "This is delicious."

"You'd be hard-pressed to screw up spaghetti," Tammy said. She chewed slowly. "It is good, though. Thank you for making dinner. It really was a long day. You know Zara, the night shift office manager? Late again. I don't know what she does, but it can't be much work. I get to the office and there are reports that haven't been reviewed and filed properly. It used to not be a problem, but with this uptick of activity that Team Mayfair has been having, it's beginning to strain me."

Rhys dropped his fork. "Oh, poor Tammy. She has to stay in the office all day and deal with people handing her paperwork for proof-reading and filing. She has to keep up with the office supplies and answer the phone or greet the clientele. It's hard for her." He stuck out his lower lip and lowered his head. "It's a tough time for you while the rest of us go out and kill zombies and then have to write about what we did."

Tammy shot him an annoyed glance, though she knew he was only joking. That was one of the reasons why she loved him: he helped put things into perspective. "I have to handle the bodies that get cremated. Do you think those just go away themselves? No, I have to make sure that the ashes get picked up and taken to another facility."

Rhys stopped mid-bite. "Those don't get scattered? We just store them somewhere else? That's disgusting."

Tammy's brows raised in surprise. "You didn't know? What, you just thought you loaded them into the oven and off they went, never to be seen again? No, we have a storage facility. I keep hearing from corporate in Nashville that they're going to bury the ashes. If that's the truth, then they better start now or else they're going to put themselves weeks behind schedule. Especially if you all continue down this very active path."

"Why hadn't I heard that?" Rhys asked, suddenly serious.

Tammy waved her hand dismissively. "You didn't know because it doesn't really concern you, does it? Part of my job is making your job easier, and that means handling the small details. I think they're going to start Project Z. That's been on the books for the last eighteen months. Those ashes should help jump start it."

"Project Z?"

"It's such a cliché name, isn't it?"

"What is it, exactly?"

Tammy took a sip from her iced tea. "They're going to start researching the zombie virus. They want to make a cure so this doesn't happen again. That's one of their goals, anyway. The other goal is to develop a test so that they just swab the mouth and see immediately if a person is infected or not. The blood test took too long to see results and was a bit too invasive."

Rhys spun his fork absently. "Why do you get to know?" he asked, skeptical.

"I'm an office manager. I know everything. People talk around us thinking we don't listen, but we do. Sometimes I call corporate for whatever reason and get put on hold, though they don't bother pressing the correct button and I can hear snippets of conversation. Of course, there's the gossip between myself and the other people who hold a similar position throughout the Divisions. That's where you get the real dirt."

Rhys' expression darkened. "You don't talk about us, do you?"

"Lighten up, Rhys. I don't tell them anything that you wouldn't want them to know. For those who spill too much, I don't repeat it. What they say doesn't leave ZRT."

"I'd feel more comfortable if you didn't say anything at all."

Tammy leaned back in her chair. "It's a give and take situation, Rhys."

"Do you talk about Elisabeth Mayfair?"

"She's a little peculiar, but I like her. Why, is there something I need to know about her? Is she not a good team leader?"

"You're being ridiculous," Rhys snapped. "She's great," he said, his tone softening. "I understand what you're telling me, but I would prefer that you not talk about our Division. We've got something we're working on and I don't want that information to spread."

"You're talking to me like I'm a fool and a water cooler gossip," Tammy said, indignant.

Rhys stood up and took Tammy's hands into his own, bringing her to his feet. "I'm sorry, honey. I didn't mean to make you feel that way." He kissed one hand gently, then the other. "How can I make it up to you?"

"Down, boy. Let me finish my dinner first."

TEAM MAYFAIR WAS gathered around the conference table, the sketches they had discovered spread out amongst them.

Amelia's forehead was knitted together, deep in concentration. "I'm going to make a wild suggestion," she said.

"By all means," Elisabeth said. "We haven't had luck otherwise. Ethan ran these through his records and came up with nothing."

"That's because they *are* nothing. The mayor and the judge are real, but the others belong to someone's imagination. We checked those zombies we brought to The Creamery and they didn't match," Amelia said matter-of-factly.

"That's a lot of faces to pluck out of an imagination," Dallas said. He was running his hands over the sketches as if he could feel the answers through the tips of his fingers.

Amelia lined up the sketches into a neat row. "What do these sketches have in common?"

The team looked at her quizzically.

"They're all good-looking." She could almost see the light bulbs ignite above their heads. "See? When you're an artist, even a creepy one like our guy, you want to draw something beautiful. You're not going to draw an ugly landscape or person. No, you're going to make them aesthetically pleasing because you want to enjoy your art and you want others to enjoy it, too."

"We've been wasting our time trying to find out if these people came from this town or anywhere else," Elisabeth murmured. "Why go through the trouble?"

"I got that one covered, too, ma'am. Whoever did this specifically wanted to waste our time."

"If it was to make sure we didn't find any more of their pop-up zombie stores, then they wasted their own time," Rhys said.

"I don't think we've found them all," Dallas replied. "I think there will be more."

"Agreed." Elisabeth swept the sketches with the palm of her hand into a manila folder. "How are the details working out for the judge and the mayor?"

"The judge is oblivious to his, but the mayor knows. Waves to him from across the street. I don't think he's upset," Rhys answered.

"The mayor has just the one detail, then?" Amelia asked, discreetly winking at Elisabeth. Elisabeth ignored her.

Rhys glanced through his notes. "Just the one. Did we need to add another?"

"Nope, he'll be all right, I'm sure." Amelia bit the inside of her cheek to stop the grin that tugged at the corners of her mouth.

"We need to look for more hideouts. We'll need to call in all teams and I want a twenty-mile search radius." Elisabeth checked her watch. "How much of the library made it through the war?"

"I think the basement was sealed off, so whatever was in there is safe. Some books were still in good condition, but a lot were used for kindling." Dallas shook his head sadly.

Amelia felt the urge to tease him, but remembered his wife had been a librarian.

"Did they keep city plans or anything that might show the schematics of town, where residents are located?" Elisabeth waited for Dallas to respond.

"A lot of that would be at the building permit office," Dallas responded. Elisabeth's face fell with disappointment; the permit office had been destroyed. Quickly, he added, "They might have some of that for genealogy. People wanted maps to see where their ancestors lived. We could try that."

"Excellent."

THIRTY MINUTES LATER, the team stood in the basement of the library. The new librarian, an older gentleman who asked to simply be called "Pecan," pulled several maps from the shelves. "These are old," he warned. "I don't know how much help they'll be. Shout if you need anything."

"Thank you, Pecan. These will be better than nothing," Elisabeth said warmly. She spread her hands over the map lying on top, its paper yellowed on the edges and ink faded. It displayed the layout of the town, minus the new construction. Dallas pulled similar maps out of the pile and they laid them on the floor, creating a miniature 2D picture.

"I'll be damned," he mused. "I didn't think we'd get this lucky."

"Believe it," Rhys said. He yanked off two bright green sticky notes from the pad Pecan had given him. Careful to not tear the maps, he put a note over the locations where they had found the hordes.

Elisabeth pointed to each spot. "They're not very close to each other. Someone has a car."

"What about the caves? Or do you think they're a coincidence?" Dallas asked.

Elisabeth frowned. "I don't know," she admitted. "The first was a direct link to the swimming hole. The second could have been used to transport bodies, but it would have been very difficult. I didn't see any tire tracks nearby when I searched."

"You could have missed them when you were playing around with the bear," Rhys said.

"I could have, but why go through the trouble of using the cave when you can more easily drive up on a road, unlock a door, and dump off a zombie? You can drop off several at a time that way. You couldn't with the cave."

"What if this is another way to throw us off?" Amelia was staring at the map, her focus as sharp as a laser.

"Who would purposely leave zombies near a cave?" Rhys asked. "Ah, son of a bitch. Same reason they made up fakes and mixed them with real people in the sketches."

Elisabeth held up her finger. "No, the first cave was on purpose. That was convenient for them and useful. I think this second location was just a holding area until they found a better place. We need to ask ourselves where are other caves located that connect to highly populated areas."

Dallas scratched the back of his head, thinking. "Appalachian Caverns. There's a mobile home park near it."

"Who lives in one of those now that they've built so many houses that are fortified?" Elisabeth asked.

"People who never left their homes, the ones that just took them with them when they became nomadic. Some returned and a few are going into an 1800s cabin style because they don't want the new home designs. The zone was cleared and they feel safe," Dallas explained.

Amelia snorted.

"Isn't that what ZRT is for? To make people feel safe?" Dallas said, his voice slightly rising.

"We know better," Amelia retorted.

"*We* might know better, but *they* don't. Would you rather have them scared and in a panic mode or content, productive citizens?"

Elisabeth thought of Ethan Brown. He would have loved to have heard Dallas now.

"My point is," Dallas said, trying to finish his thought, "Appalachian Caverns has reopened. It was a tourist attraction before and is already set up with walkways and hand rails. It's a great place. My dad took me there when I was a kid. It's big and there's another entrance somewhere. I don't know where that is, but one of the guides had said the Native Americans used it to escape raids from invading tribes."

"Is that true?" Rhys asked.

"Hell, I don't know. I do know there's a second entrance, but I don't know why it's there. Probably just because it's a natural formation and the Native American story was something to keep youngsters entertained."

"Oh." Rhys was disappointed.

"Division Tennessee will never let us blow up those caverns. Not with it being a public attraction. It would bring too much attention and Ethan won't want to explain why ZRT destroyed a perfectly good cave that people could visit for fun. The company has issued enough deceptions to last us all a lifetime." Elisabeth turned toward Dallas. "Do you remember if the guide said anything about where the other entrance is?"

"No, but I know someone who might."

HUGH ANDERSON ANSWERED the door wearing blue striped pajama pants and a matching button-up shirt. "I didn't know you were bringing guests!" he exclaimed.

"Hi, Dad," Dallas greeted his father. "You pull the security latch during the day? It's why I couldn't open the door."

"Of course I do. It's for my safety."

Dallas patted his dad on his back. "It's okay. Dad, we've got some questions for you." He pointed to the couch and recliner. "Have a seat."

The team crowded the couch while Hugh sat comfortably in his favorite chair. He pulled the handle and the bottom jutted out, lifting his feet. "Shoot."

"Dad, do you recall the Appalachian Caverns?"

"Sure I do. What about them?"

"Where's the other entrance? Do you know?"

Hugh looked out the window, trying to remember. "It wasn't anywhere close to the tourist entrance. There used to be a jail a long time ago that became a stop for local ghost tours. There was a story that one of the inmates escaped and found the cave, but got so horribly lost and died. When they were putting in the walkways and creating glow-in-the-dark guidelines for cave guides to take people on the 'extreme adventure,' they found the poor man."

"How do we know which building was the old jail?" Elisabeth asked.

"That's easy, my dear," Hugh said simply. "Look for the building with the big oak tree next to it. That's where they did the hangings."

IT WAS GETTING too dark to search for the former jail and Elisabeth decided that they would begin first thing the next morning.

She scarfed down a quick dinner when she got home and changed her clothes. She tied her training sneakers and unlocked the door to her basement.

Her basement was large and open, almost as big as the first floor of her home. The walls were painted bright white and the dark gym equipment she had acquired contrasted sharply. Her dumbbell and kettlebell racks stood side by side and her four by five rack held several more weights she used for barbell exercises. She walked across the heavy rubber mats meant to absorb high amounts of impact and went through her workout binder she had created. The bite had already made her supernaturally strong, but exercising helped maintain her fitness level and cleared her mind. She was proud of her gym, but it had to remain locked for a very good reason: no weight was below one hundred pounds. She rarely had visitors, but she didn't want anyone accidentally stumbling upon her secret.

She hopped onto her treadmill and began to run, increasing the speed every few minutes until it was maxed out and her legs were moving as swiftly as they could. Sweat beaded on her forehead and freely ran down her face. She wiped away the moisture with a towel she had thrown over the side of the treadmill.

Elisabeth was in the middle of a goblet squat when someone began banging on the basement door. She dropped the kettlebell and it landed with a loud *thud*.

As she opened the door, she used her body to block the view of her gym. "You couldn't have called first?"

Margo breezed past her sister. "Sorry," she apologized, not really meaning it. "Mom and I haven't heard from you in days."

"I've been busy."

Margo looked at the weights Elisabeth had scattered around the mats. "Circuit training?"

"I was. I'd like to get back to it."

Margo rolled her eyes. "Lizzy, you don't need to work out. The bite made sure of that."

"That's not true. I need to make sure I maintain this level of fitness."

"Have you ever stopped exercising long enough to find out if it fades?"

"No."

"Then you don't really know." She walked over to the kettlebell Elisabeth had been using and saw the amount of forty-eight kilograms printed on it. "I don't how much that is, but that's huge. Why don't you put some stuff in here that would be more suitable for someone our size?"

"That's just over one hundred and five pounds," Elisabeth said dryly. "Why would I bother? No one comes down here."

"It's good to keep up appearances," Margo said. "I'm trying to help you blend in."

"I blend in just fine. I don't need to pretend when I'm in my own home."

"You know they have dye for your irises now?" Margo said, a hint of suggestion in her voice. "With some of the things we haven't gotten back yet, here comes a company that decides people who suffered from the chemicals need to fit in more and it covers the redness. Turns their eyes brown."

"Really? How long has this company been around?" Elisabeth asked.

"Not too long. They had to do trials, needed people to be their test subjects. I don't know how many people they got with your particular condition, but they were able to make people who had normal-colored eyes have brown irises. With currency coming back, people wanted the money," Margo explained.

"How shallow."

"It's not shallow. Surely not every Abnormal works for ZRT and they're just trying to live out their lives as normally as possible."

Elisabeth knew she wasn't getting rid of her sister any time soon and began to put up her weights.

"Sorry for interrupting your workout," her sister apologized.

"You could always join me," Elisabeth offered.

Margo raised a brow. "Get real. The only thing I could use in here is that treadmill."

Elisabeth pointed to the four by five rack. "You could do pull ups," she suggested.

"I'll go the gym where I fit in. Where other men are." Margo flashed a wicked smile.

Elisabeth paused. "That's why you're here. You want to know about my date."

Margo pouted playfully. "You know me too well. How did it go? You haven't told me anything."

"It was fine."

"Oh, no. That simply will not do. 'Fine?' Elisabeth, get serious. Who do you think you're talking to?"

Elisabeth laughed and shared the details of her date with the mayor. By the time she was finished, the twins were sitting on the mats, their legs crossed like young children.

"Is he a good kisser?" Margo asked.

"Come on, now," Elisabeth said, shaking her head.

Margo said nothing.

"You're doing that trick you taught me. I'm not answering that."

Margo still said nothing.

"Damn it, fine." Elisabeth was smiling. "He's great. Is that what you wanted to hear?"

Margo grinned. "Yes! Did you invite him inside?"

"No, I didn't. That was only our first date."

"So what? You got it on with a stranger before," Margo debated.

"That was different. That was during the war."

"I see." Margo stood up. "I'm happy for you. I still don't trust the man, but that's my problem, not yours."

Elisabeth tilted her head and looked up at her sister thoughtfully. "You don't trust him or you don't trust his intentions? His intentions are to have a relationship. He actually called me the next day as he promised and we made plans for next weekend."

Margo sighed. "You know me, Lizzy. I'm protective of my baby sister."

"You're only older than I am by four minutes," Elisabeth pointed out.

"And so much the wiser for it." Margo patted Elisabeth on top of her head. "Such a young woman. We'll teach you dating etiquette soon enough."

Elisabeth rose to her feet. "If I have to learn from you, I'm in trouble," she retorted, her tone light. "What about you? Are you dating anyone?"

Margo scoffed. "I live at home with our mother. What do you think?"

"You live at home because it's safer that way. Neither of you liked it when I was there, what with my weird hours waking you up night and day and the worrying if I didn't come home immediately after a shift. If either one of us gets serious with someone, it needs to be understood that Mom will be living with one of us."

"There's no way that Mom would want to live with you," Margo said bluntly. "I didn't mean to offend you, so stop looking at me like that. She worries about you. We both do. With you on your own, it's easier for us to think of you going to work and coming home to some microwave dinner and repeating everything the next day."

Elisabeth asked, "How did you know I ate a microwave dinner tonight?"

"Oh, please. When I walked by the kitchen, I saw the box still on the counter and the smell of burnt cheese was pungent."

Elisabeth felt her cheeks redden.

"It's okay. I still love you." Margo leaned forward and hugged her sister.

Trying to change the subject, Elisabeth asked again, "Are you seeing anyone?"

"You would know it if I was. Sadly, I'm not. I'm working on a project that's taking up my extra time."

"What kind of project?"

Margo smiled mischievously. "You have your secrets and I have mine."

"You're doing an investigative piece already?"

"I told you that it's a secret. Mine may not be classified like yours, but I still can't go around blabbing my mouth to everyone."

"You're a reporter. Blabbing is your job," Elisabeth countered.

Margo raised her nose. "You say potato and I say tomato."

"That's not how that goes."

"Whatever." Margo looked toward the stairs. "I need to head home. You know how Mom gets when you leave her alone for too long after it gets dark."

Elisabeth walked her sister to the front door, watched her safely get into her car, and drive away. She still felt wired and went back to her basement to complete her workout. By the time she was finished, she had emptied her mind of the day's events and thought only of the mayor instead.

THE SUN STRAINED to shine through the dark clouds that were rolling in from the west. It had been a beautiful fall morning, but now leaves were swirling around the ground as the wind began to pick up and the temperature dropped.

Amelia Stone walked slowly through the woods, the leaves crunching beneath her boots. Her team was spread out trying to find the second entrance to the Appalachian Caves. They had found the old jail easier than they had expected, and Rhys had hoped that would be a good sign that the entrance would be just as easily discovered. That was three hours ago and Amelia decided Rhys was one of those annoying optimists. He had to be since he kept asking Tammy out despite her constant supply of negative responses.

This is getting me nowhere, she thought, frustrated. She decided to turn around and head back to the jail, a new plan on her mind. Without having to comb the surrounding woods, she was able to return fairly quickly.

The old jail had once been white with dark, metal bars where each cell had been. People mistook the bars for windows for the cells, but they really were in the chases behind them. Each block had a five-foot-wide chase that ran behind it, and the cells themselves had small, high windows that allowed in daylight. Someone had decided that prisoners should be able to have natural light for a certain number of hours—Amelia couldn't remember how many—each day yet inmates could never actually see the outside world.

Now the building was crumbling, white paint missing in chunks or having yellowed over time. Hugh had been right about the tree: it was a huge oak that loomed over the front of the property. She had imagined a noose being swung over a high branch, a group of men standing off to the side holding the slack as the executioner put the black bag over the inmate's head. Movies that showed hangings always seemed to gloss over how horrific the whole process actually was. There was a lot of gurgling as the person choked to death if his neck didn't break immediately, and they almost always left out the urine and feces that followed as sphincters loosened and released the body's contents.

The oak tree itself didn't creep out Amelia. She found it rather comforting and loved that its leaves, a yellow-gold at the moment, hadn't all fallen yet. Before the jail had been built, she imagined it had been a perfect meeting spot for young couples or families to share a picnic.

She stood in front of the tree and looked at the front of the dilapidated building. If an inmate had escaped, would he have run out the front door and kept going straight? Running straight would have led him to the town soon, and he would have been caught. No, he would have run out the back into the woods where he would have had a chance. Her team had already reached that conclusion, but she wanted to reevaluate the options.

Amelia began to run as quickly as she could, her legs carrying her down the hill from the jail and into the forest. The wind was picking up and the chill began to bite through Amelia's armor. She continued running, always taking the path of least resistance.

It began to sprinkle, the water stinging her face and eyes as she continued to run. It fell slowly at first, then, as if someone had flipped a switch, began to pour and drenched her along with her surroundings. She never slowed, even as her lungs started to burn.

The ground was uneven and she felt herself running down a small slope. She thought her experiment had failed until suddenly the ground gave out beneath her and she fell, hands reaching out to grasp anything that could stop her. Slick with moisture, the foliage slipped between her fingers and she continued to fall into a large, black hole.

She hit the bottom hard and immediately rolled out of the landing. Her momentum halted and she lay on the ground, quietly assessing any damage her body might have taken. Her knees and ankles were sore, but not sprained or broken. Her hands were cut badly and were going numb from the cold. The rest of her was, to her surprise, tender, but still okay.

Tomorrow, however, was going to be absolute hell.

"HEY, GUYS. AS much as I love being trapped underground, it would be most wonderful if one of you could find the time to come and get me." Amelia's voice was dry as it crackled through Rhys' ears.

"Where are you?" he asked.

"Marco!"

Rhys' head snapped up. "Polo!" he shouted back.

"Marco!"

"Polo!" he shouted again, walking toward the noise. Amelia's voice was heavily muffled.

"Marco!" Amelia yelled.

He was getting closer. "Polo!"

Five minutes later, he was standing over a well-concealed hole in the ground. He flipped on his flashlight and peered into the darkness. Amelia was staring back at him, her flashlight at her feet. "That's not how you play that game, you know."

"It's not? You've ruined my childhood," she replied sarcastically. "Hand me a rope and get me out of here."

Rhys looked around for a strong vine and found nothing. "Anyone got a rope? Amelia's tired of playing in her little hole," Rhys said into his throat mic.

"We've got one in the rig. I'll get it and you tell me where you are," Dallas responded.

"How in the hell did you get down there?" Rhys asked while they waited for their teammate.

Amelia shrugged. "I had a theory."

"What was that?"

"I'll explain when I get out of here."

Rhys dropped to his stomach and propped his face up on his hands. "I've got time."

"I pretended I was a prisoner who just escaped and ran until I fell in here," Amelia said.

"You're going to have to give me more than that," he replied, laughter in his voice.

"That story about the inmate who got away got me thinking. If you were going to run, you'd go where the land carried you most easily."

"Kind of like water," Rhys interrupted.

"Yes, like water. As I was saying, I wound up here."

"What'd you find?" Elisabeth asked, joining them.

"There are passageways that lead out of here, but I didn't explore farther. I'm sorry, ma'am," Amelia apologized.

"You don't want to get lost. I get it. Dallas, are you still at the vehicle?"

"Just left it," he answered.

"Go back and bring the spray paint," Elisabeth ordered.

"Ten-four," Dallas said.

"How did you wind up down there?" Elisabeth asked.

"She was playing pretend," Rhys answered. He flashed a smile toward Amelia. "She thought she wanted to be a damsel in distress."

Amelia snorted, the acoustics of where she was standing amplifying the sound. She explained to her team leader what she had done.

Elisabeth tilted her head thoughtfully. "Creative," she replied slowly. Amelia certainly knew how to think outside of the box.

Dallas arrived and tied one end of a rope around a nearby tree. The other he slung down into the hole.

"Hold that thought," Elisabeth said. "We're going to explore. Dallas, stay up here and keep watch."

"Yes, ma'am," he said.

Elisabeth looked at Rhys and winked. "Let's go play damsel in distress." She grabbed the other end of the rope and slid down it. Rhys followed closely behind her.

Inside the hole, Elisabeth shone around her flashlight. There were five passageways that ventured away from where they were standing. She instructed Amelia and Rhys to take one tunnel and spray markers along the way so that they could find their way back in case the tunnel they followed veered off again. She took another tunnel for herself.

"This one leads to a dead end," Rhys said through his throat mic. "We're going back and trying out another one."

"Okay. Be sure to mark an X next to the one you just checked."

"Doesn't that mark the spot?" Rhys asked.

"You wouldn't know the spot if it hit you in the face," Amelia retorted.

Their chattering stopped and Elisabeth continued down her path. She, too, reached a dead end. Marking an X next to the tunnel she had taken, she ventured down another. Deep into the next passageway, she wished GPS units were still available. She wanted to know where she was in regards to above ground, but she'd have to do this the old-fashioned way. "Christopher Columbus style" as Rhys had called it. They all hoped they would have access to GPS soon, though she knew it would realistically take another two to three years.

"Got something!" Amelia cried.

"What do you see?" Elisabeth demanded. She had already begun to turn around to catch up with her teammates.

"This one definitely leads to the tourist sections of Appalachian Caverns," Rhys said. "No signs of zombies."

"What about shackles or anything that would hold them down until our guy is ready to let them go?"

A pause.

"No, we see nothing. There's an underground lake here. I don't think it's very deep, though. I can see the bottom near me." Elisabeth could almost see Amelia shining her flashlight on the water by her feet.

"What about the middle?" Elisabeth was almost back to her starting point.

"Can't tell, but I think it's all the same. We'd have to get a boat."

"How do you propose we get a boat down here?" Rhys asked, incredulous.

"Get a kayak and bring it in through the main entrance," Elisabeth answered. She reached the hole where they had found Amelia, marked an O by her tunnel, and began down the last tunnel that she knew Rhys and Amelia had taken. She trekked for another thousand feet and saw the lights from the other two bobbing around the cavern.

"We could look at it now," Rhys said slowly.

Elisabeth stared at him, her expression hard.

"It would save time getting our hands on a kayak and we wouldn't have to alarm the people who own these caverns," Amelia added.

"Not you, too, Amelia," Elisabeth said, disappointed. "Damn you both," she cursed, shrugging off her weapons. She told Rhys to turn around as she removed her armor and stepped carefully into the water. It was freezing. She walked a few feet until she could go no further on her feet. Holding her flashlight in her hand, she began to swim toward the middle of the lake. It was smaller than she had initially thought and she stopped in the middle. Sticking the flashlight between her teeth, she dove underwater and the bottom rushed up to meet her. It wasn't very deep at all. Finding nothing, she began to swim back to the rocky shore.

"Turn around," Amelia said to Rhys as she saw Elisabeth swimming back to them.

Shivering, Elisabeth put on her armor and Amelia helped her with her guns. "I'm getting really tired of that. Next time, we're bringing a damn kayak and some rope with a weight on the bottom to check the depth."

"Yes, ma'am. The next time we find an underground lake after Amelia falls into a concealed hole and need to check it, I'll be sure to unhook a floatation device from my belt to use."

"I'll leave you here and not feel sorry about it," Elisabeth quipped. They were back at the entrance, and grabbing the rope, she began to climb effortlessly. Amelia and Rhys followed, Rhys not waiting for Amelia's ascent before he began his own.

Rhys reached the top and suddenly felt a tug on the rope. He turned and there was a single zombie, extremely old. It was a male and his skin was mostly gone, what organs left nothing but dried husks covered with thin, dried-beef looking bits of flesh. The zombie pulled hard on the rope and groaned. His teeth were completely exposed. *A lack of lips will do that to a man*, Rhys thought.

To Rhys' amazement, the zombie looped a section of rope around his foot and began to pull himself upward. "Holy shit!" he exclaimed.

A loud crack pierced the air and the zombie fell to the ground, his skull split open and oozing dark liquid. Rhys glanced up and saw Amelia holstering her gun.

"Damsel in distress, my ass," she told him.

SIX

Elisabeth showered once they reached The Creamery and changed into fresh clothes she kept in her locker. Rhys was in the crematorium after she had made him get back into the hole to retrieve the zombie Amelia shot. The rules of ZRT stated they could never leave behind the bodies, and she didn't want to wait for the cleanup crew to arrive for one lousy corpse.

"How did he know to climb?" Rhys had asked as he strapped the body to the top of their SUV's roof. He was aghast.

Calmly, Elisabeth had explained that the older ones displayed a higher level of intelligence. "They're not like a human, but they figure out ways to get to their food more easily the older they get."

"That wasn't taught during the safety class ZRT made me sit through," he had mumbled.

"Don't see enough old ones for them to really waste their time," Elisabeth said.

Now she was sitting in her office, busily tapping out her report of the day's events. She sent them directly to Ethan herself and waited for his phone call.

It didn't take long and she connected to him, listening to him chuckling to himself. "Have you turned into a spelunker?" he asked, snickering at his own joke.

"There's a connection here. What person is going to go wandering down a dark, unfamiliar cave? It's a perfect place to store zombies before unleashing them upon the population." She was not amused that Ethan found her activities humorous.

Noticing her tone, Ethan grew serious. "Why would someone want to send undead into gen pop?"

"I've discussed my theories with you previously."

"I was hoping that you had new ones."

"I don't. I think it's someone who wants things the way they were, before civilization rose again. Maybe—" Elisabeth cut herself off.

"Maybe what?" Ethan prompted.

"It's nothing," she murmured.

"Let me know when you've got something else." Ethan severed their connection.

Elisabeth exited her office and stood next to her team's group of cubicles. "Outside. Now."

Wordlessly, her team followed her. "Here's a theory: what would happen to ZRT if there were no more zombies?"

"Dodo bird," Amelia answered.

"Yes. ZRT has a few years while teams clear up the last of the zombies. With incidents like the rogue zombie in the cave, they'll have to go hunting rather than just sweeping regions. But if there are still zombie hordes that popped up once in a while, the fear would remain and so would the need for the company." Elisabeth put her hands on her hips, watching her team drink in the information.

"Why just here?" Dallas asked, breaking the silence.

"What do you mean?" Rhys had crossed his arms and was looking at the other man curiously.

"We would have heard of other outbreaks. We haven't, so why the isolation to just our area?" Dallas explained. "Those zombies we've been taking on are pretty fresh."

Elisabeth nodded in understanding. "I think someone already is sweeping the uncleared areas of town and they're taking the people they find, turning them, and then sending them out for us to eliminate. There are some former doomsday preppers that are still out in the wilderness who have no intention of joining the rest of the community and no one knows if they're dead or alive. Why not take advantage of the fact that we don't know who made it through the war and who didn't?

"I don't know what I'm doing after we've been told we are completely zombie-free. I haven't even thought about it. I can tell you, though, that were I one who wasn't willing to see ZRT disappear, this would be a clever strategy."

"This must be kept amongst ourselves," Elisabeth said finally.

"Don't want us to end up in a zombie pop-up store?" Rhys was smiling at her.

Quietly, she said, "No. No, I don't."

DAYS PASSED WITHOUT incident and the team was feeling restless. It was Saturday afternoon and Elisabeth was pacing back and forth in her living room, anxious. She had secretly done her own sweeps on the outskirts of town and had only eliminated less than a handful of the undead. She dumped them off at The Creamery, sneaking in through the back and stuffing the bodies inside the furnaces. She knew Team Aguilar and Team Churchill were arguing with each other about the laziness in not identifying which kills were theirs, and her additions didn't help matters. She should have said something, but she didn't want anyone to know about her sweeps and it was a little funny to watch Luke Aguilar get his feathers ruffled.

Her phone rang and she answered, expecting it to be Margo. "Hello?" she said.

"It's about time we get together, don't you think?" Elisabeth could hear the smile in Todd Wilkin's voice.

"I agree."

"Do you have anything you'd like to do?"

"Something active," Elisabeth replied. Realizing what she said, she hastily added, "Like bowling."

"Like bowling," Todd said slowly. "I've got something better. Put on your workout gear and I'll be there in an hour."

Sixty minutes later, Todd was driving Elisabeth to a place he described as being small, but helped him clear his mind. They arrived and parked in front of a brick building with large, glass windows covered with banners bearing the business name, classes offered, and schedule.

He was beaming. "I love this gym," he said. "It's a mixed martial arts gym, the only one in town. It's bigger than what it looks like on the outside. You can't get more active than this."

Elisabeth said nothing and followed him inside. He had been right; it was bigger than she initially thought. It was a large space with ceilings that were twenty feet high. Near the door was a seating area and cubby holes that reminded her of kindergarten where she and Margo had hung up their backpacks and coats. Todd pointed to a cubby, instructed her to take off her shoes, and she obliged. "You don't want to carry nasty germs in here," he said.

The floor was covered with thick, blue mats that felt smooth and plush underneath her bare feet. There was a large, metal rack that held several uppercut bags, Thai bags, and the standard punching bags. A few spots were currently occupied by sweaty men and women throwing combinations of jabs, right and left hooks, and crossover punches.

The rest of the mat was free of equipment, but on the outskirts was a small set of bleachers for additional onlookers and for people to toss their gym bags that wouldn't fit in the cubby holes. There was a full-sized boxing ring as well as, to Elisabeth's surprise, a cage in the shape of a hexagon. It was a great looking gym, almost as nice as the one where she trained for the Zombie Response Team. She hadn't told Todd yet that she had earned her purple belt in jiu-jitsu, and would have been higher had she not had to hold back her strength so that the others training wouldn't find out her condition. She had been doing really well until a large truck of a man had complained about women being in the field and that their best place was behind a desk. She had grabbed the back of his neck with her right hand and his right wrist with her left hand. She stepped her right foot onto his left hip and swung her other leg between his, causing him to tumble over her and hit the mat *hard*. She couldn't follow him to get a mounted position with that particular takedown, but had scrambled quickly back to him and threw her body across his for a side mount. She rested on the tips of her toes, driving down her chest to make herself feel even heavier. She hadn't even begun to attack his arm for a submission when he tapped and mumbled an apology.

There was another door that led to the back of the gym. It held standard equipment similar to what she had in her basement. A dock door was on the opposite side, and it was wide open to the parking lot. "The instructor doesn't run the air conditioning and rarely uses the heat. On pretty days like today, he lets them open that door to let in the fresh air because with all of this sweat, this place needs it," Todd said, appearing behind Elisabeth. "Would you like to hit some mitts? I can show you some things."

Elisabeth hid her smile and followed him back to the mats. She let him help her wrap her hands before she tightened the straps around his wrists for the mitts he was wearing.

Holding up his hands, he asked, "Do you have down your basic stance? Good, okay, let me teach you some technical punches."

"Technical punches, huh?" Elisabeth said, raising a brow.

"Sure. You can't always expect to have bullets on hand to shoot the zombies. You might have to get up really close."

Elisabeth choked back her laughter.

"Now, get into your stance and I want you to jab forward with one hand. That's good. A little bit harder than that."

Elisabeth threw a solid jab and Todd staggered backward. Obviously bewildered, he dropped his hands. Elisabeth laughed and wiped a tear from the corner of her eye.

"That's what I get for assuming you didn't know much," Todd said. "It's not that funny," he protested.

Still laughing, Elisabeth replied, "Oh, yes, it's very funny."

"I suppose I deserve that," Todd said, tearing at the Velcro around his wrists with his teeth and pulling off the mitts. He looked her up and down and added, "Gloves on, let's spar then."

"My gloves are in the side zipper compartment," she called to him as he went back to their gear.

"Elisabeth?"

Elisabeth turned around and found herself looking at Rhys. "Hi," she replied.

He looked nervous and ran his hand through his hair. "What are you doing here? Thought you had your own place for this sort of thing."

"Todd brought me," she admitted.

"The mayor? You're really dating the mayor?" He let out a low whistle. "Good for you, ma'am. I don't mean to be rude, but how long do you plan on being here?"

Elisabeth felt uncomfortable. "I'm sorry," she apologized. "I didn't mean to intrude on your personal space. I know we all need a place that we can go where we don't see people from work."

Rhys' eyes flickered toward the bathrooms. "It's not that," he said slowly.

Elisabeth followed Rhys' gaze and watched as Tammy came out of the restroom, gym bag in hand with her street clothes hanging out of the top. "Rhys!" she exclaimed.

Tammy spotted Elisabeth and froze, eyes wide. Rhys sighed and waved her over to them. "Cat's out of the bag now," he said as she approached.

"I won't tell anyone," Elisabeth said. "But why the secrecy?"

"It's a fun game for us. Keeps things fresh," Rhys answered, sliding his arm around Tammy's shoulder. "It's also funny to hear Dallas make fun of me for trying so hard." He shook his head. "If he only knew the truth!"

"Everyone makes fun of your rejected efforts," Elisabeth replied. "How long?"

"I didn't know Amelia was here with you today," Rhys joked. "It's been about eight months."

"Nine," Tammy corrected.

"Eight to nine months," Rhys said, waving his hand from side to side.

"I appreciate you keeping this a secret," Tammy said. "We'll tell people eventually, but a little bit of role play never hurt anyone."

"Whatever tickles her pickle, I do." Rhys frowned. "Everyone makes fun of me?"

"Always to your face."

He brightened. "That'll make it even better when we go public. It was nice to see you. Have fun with the mayor." He steered Tammy toward the free weights in the back room.

As they walked away, Todd returned, gloves in hand. "Can you handle the cage?" he asked, shaking the gloves.

"I can handle a lot of things." Elisabeth winked and pulled her gloves over her hand wraps.

The couple stepped into the cage and the instructor locked it behind them. The instructor, Michael Bolt, sat cage side. He was of a slight build with thinning hair, though his face read that he was only in his thirties. The schedule for that afternoon had read "Open Mat" and she noticed him when they first arrived grappling with several people, handling them easily. He had been kind and patient, explaining to them how he did different submissions when they asked, and then told them to come to class to learn more. While she enjoyed the coach ZRT provided, she wouldn't mind branching out on her own to learn from Michael.

Todd began to throw punches and she dodged them easily, keeping her own hands up and elbows by her sides. His brow knitted and Michael yelled out different numbers. He responded by throwing a series of hooks and uppercuts, though Elisabeth dodged these as well. She feigned a right kick, then switched quickly to her left leg and caught Todd in his side. He grimaced with pain, and Elisabeth felt a twinge of guilt. She wasn't using her full strength and knew she couldn't.

He shot forward, dropping to one knee, and grabbed her around her thighs, pulling her hard toward his body. She went crashing down and he released her legs, trying to take the mount position. She was too fast and brought up her legs, wrapping them around his waist and crossing her ankles so that he was in her guard. She repositioned her legs around his ribs and, with them still crossed at her ankles, began to straighten them. She leaned forward to hug around her own thighs and Todd blanched. She was crushing him and he looked at the instructor for help.

Michael's eyes were wide and he began to laugh. "I haven't seen a huggy bear in years!" he cried. "Might as well tap. I can't believe she got you in that." He was now standing by the side of the cage, his hands wrapped around the fence. "Wow, that's great."

Todd tapped and Elisabeth released him. "I guess I should have known ZRT would teach you stuff, but why would they teach *that*? When would you ever do that to a zombie?" He stood to his feet, rubbing his aching ribs.

"You should have tapped sooner," Elisabeth said lightly.

"Listen to the lady," Michael chimed in. "Ready for another round?"

Todd was taking off his gloves, ignoring the instructor.

Elisabeth frowned. She had hurt his pride. She moved next to him and quietly apologized. "I'm sorry. I thought you were up for that."

"I wasn't up for losing," he snapped.

Elisabeth motioned for Michael to unlock the cage. She wasn't interested in the mayor's childish behavior. As he did, a scream ripped through the air. Michael paused and turned toward the sound. "I'll be right back to get you. I need to check on that." He ran toward the back room.

Elisabeth smelled them first. They were coming in through the dock door that other people were desperately trying to close. She could hear a gun firing and knew that was Rhys; no one at ZRT was ever too far away from a weapon.

She grasped onto the cage and launched herself upward. Todd grabbed her leg. "What are you doing?" he demanded.

"My job," she said.

"You don't have anything. Let them call ZRT and get another team out here. We're safest here, in this cage."

Ignoring him, Elisabeth swung herself over the side and ran toward the screaming. She pointed at a teenager huddled on the bleachers. "You, call ZRT now! Tell them to send a cleanup crew, too!"

The teenager raced across the mats, grabbed the phone by the front desk, and began to punch in the numbers.

Elisabeth rushed into the back room to find Rhys firing, Tammy feeding him spare magazines. "How many do you have left?"

"I only have two spares!" he shouted over the noise.

That won't be enough, she thought. She glanced around the room at all of the witnesses. She didn't have a choice. She grabbed a barbell off the rack and flung it across the room like a spear. A zombie's skull caved inward and it fell, knocking down a few zombies that were behind it.

She went to the dumbbell rack and began to throw them one by one at the incoming undead. They fell as their brains imploded, and soon she had moved onto the kettlebells. These were harder to throw, so she grabbed the heaviest one and used it as a hammer. She ran from zombie to zombie, bashing in their heads and quickly moving on to the next one.

The sound of Rhys' 9mm stopped and Elisabeth yelled for him to get the people still alive to a safe place. Tammy clapped her hands loudly and Rhys shouted, "Follow me if you want to live!"

Tammy groaned. "Really? Now?"

He winked at her.

Tammy led the group and Rhys followed, waiting until the last person alive ran past and he pulled up the back.

The kettlebell Elisabeth had been using was sticky with blood and she used it one last time, leaving it on top of an undead cranium. She was out of equipment to throw and found the barbell she had tossed earlier. She picked it up and removed the weights from each side. Holding it like a bat, she swung it easily. Objects began to fly and she realized she was using all of her strength and was actually knocking *off* their heads. They sprayed blood and other fluids as they spun through the air, covering the walls. There was a wall with a mirror that Elisabeth hadn't noticed initially and she saw herself, drenched in blood, bits of bone, and brain matter.

There were no more zombies, but there were several people slouched against the walls and across the floor. She touched them all to be one hundred percent certain, but she could already tell by their scent that they were going to turn. She'd have to check the others Rhys had led away, too.

"I guess that answers my question," said a voice next to her.

"So much for the secret," she said solemnly.

Luke Aguilar nudged her arm. "It's okay. I like knowing one of you is on our side."

"I'm not the only one."

"I know that, too. My team and I won't tell anyone else, though I will tell Ethan to stop bullshitting me."

Elisabeth was staring at the people around the room. They were barely breathing. "Did you bring the syringes?"

"Ambulance is on its way."

"It's too late for these people."

"All of them?" He shook his head.

"All of them," Elisabeth confirmed. "I don't need to do a field test."

"Figured that, too," Luke said, his voice sad. He reluctantly removed the syringes and handed them to her. He watched as Elisabeth went to each one and soothingly told them they would be all right. She reassured them again as she plunged in each needle and didn't budge from their sides until she was sure that they were dead.

Her heart was heavy as she went out to the front of the building, Luke by her side. A small crowd had gathered in the parking lot. The rest of Luke's team was making sure no one left while the emergency medical technicians set up their mobile unit.

Some were chatting excitedly amongst themselves while others complained that they wanted to leave. "No one is going anywhere," Luke boomed. "We need to check everyone out and then you will be free to go."

A hush fell over the crowd and they lined up for the EMTs to check on them.

"What a commander," Rhys said in wonderment.

Elisabeth glanced at him out of the side of her eyes.

"I still would prefer you any day, ma'am."

"Thank you," she said quietly. "And thank you for earlier."

"I was just doing my job," he replied. "Tammy and I are going to help Team Aguilar keep these people in line. Cleanup crew is here. They parked in the back so they don't alarm anyone." Lowering his voice, he added, "I don't think anyone really saw you in action. Adrenaline surges have been used for ages to explain sudden bouts of strength if they did."

"Thank you," she repeated. She walked over and stood next to Luke. "We have an issue," she whispered.

"Infection?"

"Not all of them. Just one."

"That shouldn't be an issue."

Elisabeth frowned. "It's the owner," she replied miserably.

Oh," Luke said simply. "Which one?" Elisabeth discreetly pointed to Michael Bolt's smaller form and Luke approached him, careful to not let Michael touch him. "I'm going to need you to come with us," he said.

Michael nodded. "Of course. You want some sort of statement."

"Yes."

He followed Luke and Elisabeth and motioned for them to join him in his office. He took a seat behind his desk and Elisabeth shut the door. "I was unlocking the cage door when I heard a scream," he began.

"You're infected," Elisabeth said bluntly.

Michael blinked several times, uncomprehending. "No, I can't be. I don't have a scratch or bite on me. We all checked each other after that couple led us away."

"Blood could have gotten into your mouth or eyes," Elisabeth explained.

"You didn't do a test. This just happened! How could you possibly know?" Michael began to cry, his large, hot tears freely flowing down his face.

"It's our job to be able to tell these things," Luke answered steadily.

"I worked so hard for all of this," he said, spreading his hands as if encompassing the building. "I wanted a place for people to learn, to work, and to feel normal after the war. Are you sure?" When he didn't receive an answer, he slumped in his chair, defeated.

"We're going to put you in quarantine. You'll have a chance to set up paperwork to leave this to someone else. Your dream doesn't have to die with you," Luke said.

"I know someone," Michael choked. He suddenly reached forward and grabbed Elisabeth's hands. "Thank you. Thank you for letting me say my goodbyes."

THE FIGURE HAD joined the crowd and ignored the person who asked when it had changed clothes. It watched Elisabeth walk inside with another team leader whose name it couldn't remember as well as a person it did not recognize. Elisabeth looked professional, though the figure knew inside that she was distraught.

It had stuffed as many zombies as it could onto a bus and dropped it off nearby the gym. It waited until the last undead got off and it drove away, driving normally so that it wouldn't draw attention to itself. It ditched the bus a few blocks over and returned to the gym, sunglasses on and hood up to cover its hair. It hated to put Elisabeth in pain, but she would learn soon enough that it was all necessary.

Noticing Rhys and the office manager, Tammy, the figure slowly backed away before turning around completely and heading back in the direction from whence it came.

ELISABETH STOOD BY the wall and watched the cleanup crew collect the bodies and zip up the black plastic bags. Some were already being hauled away and, once all of the bodies were gone, would be returned to The Creamery. A few members of the crew were already busy scrubbing down the gym to remove the gore. Disinfectant would soon cover every inch of every surface.

Luke had taken Michael away to quarantine where he would get his affairs in order. Elisabeth would get in trouble for going against protocol, but she was prepared to set the phone aside while Ethan yelled.

With the last body bag gone, she walked out to the parking lot where Todd was waiting. Rhys had already apologized for not noticing him sooner to get him out of the locked cage. "In my defense, he could have climbed out like you did," Rhys had said.

"Do you have different clothes?" Todd asked, his nose crinkled.

Elisabeth looked down at herself. She knew she looked grotesque and she stank of foulness she never could have imagined as a child. "Would fresh clothes do me any good?" she asked.

Todd shifted his weight back and forth between each foot, thinking. "I've got an old blanket in the back that you can sit on."

"How gracious," Elisabeth replied, trying to hide her sarcasm.

The two rode back to Elisabeth's house in silence. When they arrived, he told her, "I'll call you soon."

Elisabeth knew he wouldn't keep his promise this time, nor did she care.

FRESHLY SHOWERED, ELISABETH lay in her bed, exhausted. She thought about the poor gym owner and the people she'd had to eliminate. If scientists were going to research anything, they could at least look for a cure.

She curled onto her side and closed her eyes, trying to find an inner peace to help her sleep.

A window shattered and her eyes flew open. Her house was fortified and would take a great force to break inside. Instantly, she was sitting up, her hand reaching under her pillow for her Smith and Wesson.

Several men entered her room and, without preamble, shot her in her shoulder. She cried out in pain and fell backward. One man dug his fingers into her wound while another slammed a taser gun into her side and pulled the trigger.

The rest of the men swiftly zip-tied her hands and feet together and clumsily picked her up. One laughed mirthlessly as he shoved his thumb into the bullet hole again and withdrew it. Unbeknownst to them, Elisabeth could already feel her wound closing and briefly thought of Rhys asking her if she could survive a gunshot. She had told him about Margo shooting her by accident years ago, but he had smiled sadly and said softly, "I meant somewhere that could do real damage." He had pointed to her heart and then her head, muttering that he hoped they would never have to find out.

Her thoughts raced. What should she do? She made up her mind quickly.

The electricity was still jolting through her and she gritted her teeth in pain. It did hurt, but she wiggled her body to make them think it was worse than it actually was. She pretended to struggle against the zip ties and one of the men laughed. "She's got her limits," he said, his voice full of glee.

Elisabeth allowed them to dump her in the trunk of a car and drive her away. Soon, they were at their destination and one of her assailants shoved a potato bag over her head.

"A potato bag?" she heard one ask.

"All I had," came a grunted response.

They yanked her out of the trunk by her arm and picked her up again, not risking what would happen if they cut the zip ties. She could barely see out of the bag and she felt herself being carried up some stairs before the land plateaued.

A door opened and she heard footsteps pounding against the floor, echoing off the walls around her.

Another door opened and they stopped, setting her down in a chair. Two men tied her wrists to the arms of the chair. She heard the men leave her side, but they didn't go far. They were lining the walls of the office to which they'd taken her.

A low voice that sounded like it was gargling gravel said, "You are quite the find."

"Am I?" Elisabeth asked, pretending to sound fearful. "What do you want?"

"Why you, of course. Blood, tissue samples, the works. We can study you, learn how to make ourselves like you. What makes you tick, tick, tick."

Elisabeth didn't respond, waited for the man to continue.

"We'll take your sister. Margo, is it? See if we can duplicate the bite in her. It's too bad you aren't triplets. I could have one bitten and the other injected with your blood and see which one causes the mutation to being an Abnormal. If the mutation is even based off DNA alone."

Elisabeth ceased pretending to be afraid. "No," she said firmly.

She could hear the man lean forward, his chair squeaking. "You forget that you're in no position to argue with me."

She snapped her head up and ripped her arms from their bonds. She pulled her feet apart and the zip ties broke easily. She yanked off the potato sack and threw it to the ground. She stared at the man in front of her. "We need to have a chat," she said angrily.

One of her assailants rushed forward and tried to stick his finger in her wound. Confusion crossed his face as he realized that it was gone and she grabbed him by his throat. She lifted him off the ground a few inches before slamming him back down. His head bounced against the floor upon impact. She bent over and grabbed a handful of hair and smashed his head once more into the floor and the man went limp.

She straightened and looked at the remaining men. Her gaze locked with one. "You're the one who jammed his finger into my bullet hole. Unfortunately for you, you answered my own question."

His hand rested on top of his side arm. "What question is that?"

Elisabeth lashed out quickly, her fingernails slicing through the man's neck. His head didn't separate but hung limply to the side by a few tendons. "Getting my blood on you *will* infect you." Eyes widened, the other men decided to avoid the risk of shooting her. Instead, they jumped on her at once and she was crushed beneath a pile of bodies trying to pin her.

Teeth gnashing, she bit into soft flesh and tore out chunks without discretion. Bright red arterial blood filled her mouth as she realized she had severed a brachial artery. Tenth grade biology taught her that he'd bleed out quickly, and she moved onto the next attacker. This one kicked her in her ribs and she felt them crack. Ignoring the pain, she thrust out the heel of her hand and smashed it into his sternum. She heard it shatter, and a piece of it pierced his heart. He dropped to the ground in a heap.

She unclipped a weapon from the next foe. "You brought a revolver?" she asked, incredulous.

"It's my favorite," the man replied simply. He took a step forward and she threw his firearm. It hit him in his temple and she used the distraction to rake her nails across his chest. Skin separated from muscle and he dropped to his knees. He desperately tried to reattach the skin by pressing it over his bloody gashes. Elisabeth grabbed the revolver from the floor and shot him with his own gun, then turned to face the last assailant.

He held up his hands in defense. "I'm going to walk away. I'm sorry," he apologized. Elisabeth wrapped her hands around his wrist and squeezed, felt his bones break beneath her grip.

She leaned in close and whispered in his ear. "I accept your apology."

Then Elisabeth ripped out his throat.

SEVEN

For the second time that day, Elisabeth found herself covered in blood and gore. She kicked a body out of the way and dragged a chair over to the front of her kidnapper's desk. She sat in it, casually swinging one leg over the other.

"How long did you know that it was me?"

Elisabeth pointed at her nose. "The sense of smell is very much underrated."

The man steepled his hands. He had stopped trying to disguise his voice. "Where do we go from here?"

"I'm not interested in seeing you anymore," Elisabeth said easily.

Mayor Todd Wilkins nodded his head. "I wasn't going to call you."

"I know. The sore loser trait doesn't suit anyone."

"At least I know why I lost when we sparred," he replied, indignant.

Elisabeth snickered. "I would've beaten you even if I didn't have this condition."

"Let's agree to disagree, then."

"All right." Elisabeth rushed out of her seat and around the desk. Todd cowered back in his chair. "What in the *fuck* did you think you were going to do with me?" she demanded.

"I saw you at the gym. Your colleague thought we were all outside, but I was worried about you. I went back inside to help and saw you didn't need any. You were amazing," he said, full of awe.

"While I appreciate the compliment, I do not appreciate being taken against my will and I sure as hell am not fond of you threatening my family." She pointed to her shoulder. "I also really hate being shot."

The mayor raised his brows. "You got shot and it healed?"

Elisabeth glared at him.

"You weren't taken against your will," he corrected. "You had my men fooled on that account."

Elisabeth shook Todd's chair and he cringed. "How many people did you tell?"

"Just the ones that you killed already."

She slid a fingernail over her left arm, making herself bleed. She dipped the same finger into the crimson liquid and held it by Todd's eye. "Why don't you think about that again?"

He was shaking violently. "I swear, I told no one else!"

"What about the scientists you were going to have treat me like a lab rat?" she asked.

"I just told them to expect something special. I didn't tell them what. I promise, no one else knows about you."

She wiped her finger on her shirt and paused, suddenly aware that she was only wearing a long green T-shirt and blue underwear.

"What are you going to do with me?" Todd asked. He looked nervously around his office full of bodies, some which were still intact and others that weren't.

"We're going to The Creamery."

Elisabeth arrived at The Creamery wearing Todd's pants with his belt buckled at the tightest hole. She dragged Todd alongside her, and Luke Aguilar catcalled at his yellow-striped boxers.

"Bringing your dates back to the office?" he asked.

"Call in my team and Churchill's," she ordered. "And meet me down at quarantine. How fast can Ethan Brown get here by helicopter?"

Luke stopped and noticed Elisabeth's appearance and expression. "Is he infected? How did you not notice it earlier?"

"He's not infected," Elisabeth answered. "Just do what I asked for and I'll explain later. Please tell Amelia to bring me extra clothes. I don't think that I have any more in my locker."

"I'm on it," he responded and started barking orders at the rest of his team.

Elisabeth opened the door to the stairs and held it for Todd to walk through first.

"Ladies first," he said.

"I'm not walking in front of you. Move your ass."

He grumbled as he shuffled past her and began his descent. Two flights down and they reached the heavy, locked door to quarantine. She punched in her code and they entered a long hallway lined with Plexiglas walls. On each side were many smaller enclosures that housed a twin bed, desk, and a chair. Todd could see someone at the end pressing his face against the glass, trying to see who was coming.

Elisabeth stopped next to Michael Bolt's cell and entered another code. A door swung open and she gestured for Todd to go inside. He held up his hands defensively. "I'm so sorry, Elisabeth. I overreacted. I should never had done that to you."

Elisabeth said nothing and shut the door, heard it lock automatically.

"Can I get something to drink?" Todd shouted through the glass.

Still ignoring him, Elisabeth went into Michael's cell. "How are you?" she asked, her body blocking the doorway.

Michael sat on the bed, his knees drawn to his chest. "I'm going to die."

"I wish I could have saved you sooner," she said softly.

"Are you sure I'm not like you?" he asked.

"Positive."

"Oh," he said simply.

"We're going to have a lawyer here tomorrow to draw up a will for you. It'll make it easier for your successor."

"Thank you." He pointed at the books scattered on top of his desk. "Thank you for the reading material as well."

"Did you give the list of people you want to see to Rhys?"

"I did," he replied, hanging his head. "You know," he began quietly, "I should have died a long time ago. I accepted it then. I was trapped in an attic and the windows were stuck shut. They had some steel bars on them, so I couldn't just kick them out. The zombies hadn't found the pull-down ladder I had yanked back into the ceiling. But they had learned that they could make a pile of themselves and reach the ceiling and starting clawing through it." He shook his head slowly. "People think drywall is so strong. It's not. They were starting to come up *through* the ceiling and I just knew my time was up. But I kept trying to pull on that window and it finally broke free. I threw it up and climbed out onto the roof and jumped down on the ground. They were still working on getting into the attic when I found a skateboard of all things to escape. That skateboard is still in my office.

"When we won the war, or so I thought we had until today, I wanted to do something positive. I wanted to pass on my years of martial arts training to the next generation. I don't know how to farm or how to fix things, but this, *this* is something I could do to help. I love coaching, the way a student's eyes light up when they learn something new. I love the self-confidence that martial arts provides. If I hadn't had training, I might have stopped pulling at the window. Just given up. But I was taught to never stop trying until you succeed and, when you do succeed, keep practicing because you can only get better."

Elisabeth leaned forward and patted his knee gently. "Thank you for sharing that with me."

"Yeah," he said, his voice thick.

"Let me know if you need anything. Whatever you want." Elisabeth closed the door behind her and started down the hallway.

"Hey!" the mayor shouted. "You can't just leave me in here. I'm the mayor! You said yourself that it would be bad if something happened to me!" He pounded his fists against the glass.

His only response was silence.

"ETHAN BROWN IS on his way," Amelia said. She stood outside the locker room showers, her back to her team leader. "What happened to you?"

Amelia heard the water shut off. "I'll explain when everyone is together." Elisabeth wrapped herself in a towel and walked out of the shower, her bare feet padding against the floor. "Thanks for getting me some more clothes. I used up my last set the other day and was going to replace them this week. Didn't expect to need them so fast."

"No problem, ma'am," Amelia replied. "How are things with the mayor?" she asked, trying to change the subject.

"He's a dead man," Elisabeth answered. She pulled her pale blue sweater over her head and zipped her jeans. "Jeans?" She pointed at her legs.

"It's Saturday night. Don't worry. It's only the ZRT Director of Division Tennessee that will be here," Amelia said flippantly.

"Mm-hmm," Elisabeth murmured. She ran a comb through her damp hair and decided to French braid it. Sliding one strand over another, she said, "I'll meet you in the conference room."

Elisabeth finished dressing and met her team, along with Team Aguilar and Team Churchill. They were talking amongst themselves around the large conference table when she entered the room. They ceased speaking at the sight of her. "When will Ethan be here?" she asked.

"Five minutes," Dallas answered.

"Your information is outdated." Ethan Brown walked into the room, his two body guards flanking him. He looked over the crowd, his gaze resting on Elisabeth. "You better have a damn good reason for summoning me to East Tennessee."

"You mentioned once before that I was lucky myself and others like me hadn't been turned into experiments," Elisabeth began. "Are there people with my condition being studied?"

Ethan's eyes flickered around the room and he hesitated.

"You're still worried about my condition being a secret?"

"Yes," Ethan answered.

"Too late." Luke Aguilar flashed a smile. "Oh, come off it, Ethan. Things like that shouldn't be kept a secret amongst colleagues in this business."

"Are there people with my condition being studied?" Elisabeth repeated, redirecting Ethan's attention.

"Yes, there are," he replied.

A few people gasped and Luke shushed them.

"How many?" Elisabeth demanded.

"I don't know why you're getting your panties in a wad. They're all volunteers."

"Really? Because tonight I almost became a 'volunteer.'" Elisabeth held up her fingers to make air quotes.

"What are you talking about? We are doing experiments, but we've asked for volunteers. We ask the people that aren't working for us because we don't want to risk Abnormal employees getting injured when we need them in the field. We call it Project Z." Ethan propped his arms on the back of an empty chair and leaned forward, his posture casual. A few snickered at the project's name and Ethan shot them a look of contempt. They quieted immediately.

"What did you do, Ethan? Offer them a job at ZRT and then haul them off to an unknown location if they turned you down?"

"Don't be ridiculous, Elisabeth," Ethan warned. "We draw blood, take some tissue samples. We've been infecting rats with their blood to see if they can infect others."

"I can already tell you the blood is infectious, but other bodily fluids aren't," Elisabeth said flatly.

He raised his brows. "Ah, a little freelancing in your free time? We'll confirm the results in the laboratory."

"What else are you testing for?" Dallas asked.

Ethan addressed the rest of the room's occupants. "We want to know what it is that makes people like Elisabeth the way they are. We want to know if it's isolated to DNA or if it's something else special about a person that turns them into an Abnormal. Can we pinpoint specific aspects of the condition and give the rest of us things like super strength and healing? We've already discovered that the longer someone lives with the condition, the more rapidly they heal. I would like that; wouldn't you?"

Amelia interjected. "You talk about DNA. You're looking for identical twins." She wasn't asking a question.

"We would like to have that option, yes. Again, though, we're only interested in volunteers."

"Is everyone on the board of directors in agreement? Or is it a split decision?" Rhys asked timidly.

"There are some who don't want to wait for volunteers to come forward, meaning it is a majority rules situation," Ethan answered. He straightened. "We're not doing anything underhanded. We're trying to better the human race. We're not going to do that through intimidation or force. We might offer incentives down the road if we can't get enough volunteers."

Elisabeth watched him warily. "What do you know about rogue labs?"

"There should be no one but ZRT staff working on this particular project. We can control the regulations better this way and that frees up other scientists that survived to work on cures or treatments for other ailments." He paused. "Then there are those who are more interested in beauty regimes," he added bitterly. "What a waste of brilliance."

Elisabeth chose her next words carefully. "What will happen to ZRT when teams eradicate the zombies?"

"We'll exist as a precaution, greatly reduced of course. Most likely switch to being a research company instead," Ethan answered honestly.

"We have a working theory," Elisabeth said slowly. Her team began shaking their heads and she stopped.

"What's your theory?" Ethan asked, curious.

"Ethan," she started, her voice heavy. "Would someone in ZRT be in disagreement with a new direction for the company and purposely plant hordes of zombies to keep us relevant?"

Shocked, Ethan spat, "Preposterous!"

"Then explain why the sudden influx in hordes. We think people are being turned that stayed away from the safe zones, the ones who were the doomsday preppers. They wouldn't be missed by an established community that had been cleared."

"Elisabeth, we need to have this discussion in private," Ethan said quietly.

"No, you need to have this discussion now, in the open," Dallas snapped.

The others in the room looked at Ethan expectedly.

"Have you forgotten who the boss is?" Ethan's cheeks flushed red with anger. "It's me in case you needed the reminder."

"We'll talk," Elisabeth agreed. "I want team leads Luke Aguilar and Nicholas Churchill with me, though."

"You've got a pair of balls on you today, don't you?" Ethan sighed. "Fine." He led them to Elisabeth's office, and sat in her chair. "You need to understand that you are the only region with these outbreaks. Everywhere else is already being downsized because of inactivity. It will be a slow process, but team members are being relocated to other departments within ZRT, or if ZRT cannot find somewhere for them to go, we set them up with another company."

"Why us?" Nicholas asked. Elisabeth looked at him. His bushy mustache wiggled when he spoke, but his voice was so soft that a person had to strain to listen to him.

"I don't know, but we have discussed sending displaced team members here to help with the problem."

"Why couldn't you tell us this in front of everyone else?" Nicholas pressed.

"Because we have the same theory as you do about people being turned. We, too, think they're people outside the safe zones. We also think that someone in your region found out about the shrinking of ZRT and they're creating the undead on purpose. *That's* why I couldn't talk to you in front of the rest of your teams. We don't want to risk a potential threat knowing that we're secretly investigating everyone.

"No one on Team Aguilar would make a zombie," Luke said angrily. "We've lost husbands, wives, parents, grandparents, and children. No one would be willing to jeopardize losing more people they love just to keep a goddamn job."

Nicholas was nodding vigorously. "The same goes for Team Churchill."

"That's all of us," Elisabeth agreed. "Each of us has lost too much."

"I'm sorry, but the investigation will continue. I know you have a close bond with your teams, but we need to be sure."

"You don't have any other ideas as to why there are created hordes?" Elisabeth asked.

Ethan shook his head. "We just know they're being created. Another working theory is that someone is just plain evil."

"Evil? That's the best you've got?" Luke asked, frowning.

"People were evil before the war. Who's to say they wouldn't be after it?"

"Ah, evil," Elisabeth interjected. "I have one of them in quarantine."

"I understand it's the mayor," Ethan said. "I also understand that he's not infected." He stared at Elisabeth pointedly.

She quickly explained that night's events.

Luke and Nicholas exchanged glances. "I think the director was wrong about Elisabeth. We can agree that Todd Wilkins has the biggest set of balls on him this evening," Luke murmured.

Nicholas stifled a laugh.

Annoyed, Ethan looked at the men before addressing Elisabeth. "That does explain why you grilled me about rogue labs."

"Yes, and I'd like to think that you would do something about these labs that won't be so patient and wait for volunteers."

"Of course we'll search for those labs. Again, I think this might be another isolated incident. We need to speak with the mayor," Ethan said.

The team leaders got up and Ethan followed them, waving off his guards. They were soon in quarantine and standing inside the mayor's cramped quarters.

Todd eyed Ethan Brown. "You're the man in charge, I see." Receiving no reply, he continued. "Do you have any idea what kind of wild animal you have working for you? She needs to be locked up, examined. My people can help. They're willing to do more than what your people are." He flashed a smile, drawing on his political charm. "How good would that make you look to find a cure for the zombie virus? Or make the human race even better? We need people like her."

"Our labs will make those discoveries with a clear conscious," Ethan said simply.

Todd gaped. "You can't be serious. We can't make the advancements we desperately need by following all of the rules. I'm not saying we should kill these Abnormals." He practically spat out the word *Abnormal.* "I'm saying we keep them where we can have twenty-four-hour access." He pointed to his cell. "Somewhere nicer than this place. A toilet with some privacy, for one."

"Are you the only one running an independent research facility?" Ethan asked.

Todd jutted out his chin, defiant.

Elisabeth grasped his shoulder and forced him to sit on his butt. "Answer him," she said steely.

"I'm not afraid of you, bitch. You won't hurt me in front of your superior." Todd smirked.

Ethan threw a hard right and it landed squarely on Todd's jaw. "Mr. Mayor, I would suggest that you reevaluate your circumstances. You forget that you're in the presence of ZRT, an Abnormal, and most importantly, *me.*"

Rubbing his jaw, Todd retorted, "Everyone has a superior. Even you."

"There are forty-eight other Division Leaders that make up the board. No one is above another, but my equals would agree with me in regards to you."

"Forty-eight?" Todd asked.

"Yeah, we gave up on Hawaii during the war. It was too infested with zombies and too remote to even try to save. We bombed it," Ethan answered.

Elisabeth hadn't been disappointed when she heard Hawaii had been eco-bombed and there weren't even islands left to inhabit in the future. She had gone on vacation in high school with her family and found the locals to be rude. The other beaches were littered with trash when they tried to escape the overly crowded and downright stinky Waikiki Beach. She was glad she couldn't go back with her new senses. The smell of urine and sunscreen at Honolulu's most famous sandbox was overpowering even then.

"Are you the only who knows about the lab?" Nicholas asked.

Todd wearily looked at them. "There's only one place, but I have a partner. Or maybe I have more than one partner. That I cannot tell you."

"You need to review your situation," Ethan warned.

"I'm the mayor. You can't let anything happen to me. It would cause too much panic."

Ethan smiled mirthlessly. "I can keep you down here for as long as I need. We'll churn out a bogus scandal and call for an emergency election."

"You don't have the power," Todd replied. He was unsure of himself.

"You're quite mistaken. We're leaving now and you think about giving us the names of your partners. If you want to remain as the mayor, I suggest you give us the answers we seek by this time tomorrow. We'll let you live, but you will be watched."

Back in Elisabeth's office, she was staring at her Division Leader. "You'll really let him live?"

Ethan looked at her evenly. "No. You're going to kill him."

EIGHT

Valerie Castle was cunning, tall, slender, and beautiful. She was also Division Tennessee's mouthpiece. She ran a lint roller over her blue pencil skirt, adjusted her white blouse, and gently touched the sides of her perfectly coifed hair. She knew how she looked, but she knew that wasn't the only reason ZRT hired her. She carried an air of confidence most people dreamed about, and her presence commanded respect and trust. In other words, people found it hard to distrust her.

She dropped the lint roller into her red leather tote bag. Pushing back her shoulders, she left the bathroom and walked down the hallway toward the press room, her high heels clicking against the floor. She moved at a brisk pace and was soon standing outside of a heavy wooden door. She could hear chattering inside as they waited for her big announcement. Taking a deep breath, she opened the door and the reporters immediately fell silent. All eyes were on her as she stepped in front of the podium and placed her perfectly manicured hands on each side of it.

"Thank you all for coming," she began, her voice crisp. "I'll get right to it: last night, a field test alerted us to the infection of Mayor Todd Wilkins."

Questions erupted. Valerie pointed to a man in a striped suit. "Yes?" she prompted.

"Why didn't the field test come back sooner after the attack at the gymnasium?" the suited man asked.

"In the chaos of yesterday's events, we believe he switched tests with another individual that was present," she answered coolly. "Yes, you," she said, pointing to another reporter.

This one was plump, her hair piled haphazardly on top of her head. "How could he have done that?" she demanded. "What about the person he switched the tests with?"

"As I stated previously, yesterday's events were chaotic. We believe that he took advantage of the ZRT personnel being distracted as they tested the multiple individuals involved, and that is when he made the swap with the samples they had already collected.

"To address your question regarding the individual we have taken to quarantine: we will administer another field test to ensure that person is infection-free before issuing a release."

"Why are the labels so easily removed and replaced?" shouted a male voice from the back of the room.

"We have labels on which we write names and then they are placed over the test tubes. After yesterday's debacle, I can assure you that we will be changing protocol."

More shouting, more questions.

Valerie raised her hands slightly and the press quieted once again. "Within the next thirty days, we will be holding an emergency election to replace Mayor Todd Wilkins. We encourage everyone to vote and I thank you again for your time," she concluded. Ignoring the onslaught of additional questions, she removed herself from the room.

She turned left and walked until she reached the mayor's office. She entered quietly, the smell of blood assaulting her nostrils. "It's done," she said simply.

The director of ZRT Division Tennessee inclined his head toward her. "Thank you, Valerie."

Valerie's eyes flickered over the office as she watched a cleanup crew remove the bodies. Some were missing parts and she noticed one crew member who had the specific task of making sure limbs or heads went to the correct torso. It didn't even phase her. "We could have had a bit more flair to the story. I miss the good scandals of the old days."

"Oh, yes, some of those were outrageous, weren't they? I think my favorite was the president's wife being caught in bed with a well-known terrorist." He smiled at the memory. "What an example they made of her treason!"

"She was locked away, quite comfortably I may add, in a cell in upstate New York. When the war broke out, someone let in a zombie and there was nothing left of her afterward."

Ethan turned away from watching the cleanup crew, his expression shocked. "Really? Even *I* didn't know that. How did you?" Ethan paused, shook his head. "Former White House Chief of Staff."

"I don't know that because of my previous position," Valerie replied. She met his gaze, her red eyes twinkling. "I was the one who released the zombie into the First Lady's cell."

Ethan cleared his throat. "Good job, Valerie. Please head back to ZRT and wait for me. We'll return to Nashville together."

"Yes, sir."

ELISABETH SAT AT her desk, staring at her notes. Her vision was blurring and she blinked several times to clear it. She hadn't slept all night. After Ethan went to his hotel—the only one available in Pine Valley—she had recounted their conversation to the rest of the team members. She left out the theory that one of them was purposely turning and releasing zombies and that they were all being investigated. Rhys had thanked her privately that she never mentioned Tammy's presence at the gym during the debriefing.

She wondered how the press conference had gone. Ethan had called in the mouthpiece, a woman she had heard of, but never met. It was Valerie who had personally delivered the lies to the media regarding Abnormals. She repeated whatever Ethan wanted, and she did her job very well.

There was a soft knock on her door, and Elisabeth looked up. She blinked several times again, startled.

A tall woman stood in her doorway, a red tote slung casually over her shoulder. She dropped the tote into a chair and held out her hand.

Elisabeth grasped it, finding it cool to the touch. "Elisabeth Mayfair," she introduced herself.

"Valerie Castle," the woman replied. "I see our fearless leader failed to mention something very important."

"Yes, he did." Elisabeth peered curiously into Valerie's red eyes that matched her own.

Valerie laughed easily. "I can't believe the public bought the chemical story. That explanation wasn't my favorite."

"There were options?"

Valerie sat in a chair, and casually crossed one long leg over the other. She leaned back, draping one arm over the back of the seat. "There are always options. I have an opinion, but it boils down to whatever it is that Ethan wants."

"Does anyone else in Nashville know about your condition?"

"Just a few. I imagine it's the same for you here, isn't it?"

"It's more common knowledge lately," Elisabeth admitted.

"Ah, special circumstances of your little situation," Valerie surmised.

"I don't know if it's a 'little situation.'"

"Of course I didn't mean that literally. You're smart, you're an excellent leader. People talk. I listen," Valerie said carefully.

"You sound like Tammy, our office manager."

"They do seem to know a lot, don't they?" Valerie chuckled. "I know you want to know why I'm not a team leader."

"The thought crossed my mind," Elisabeth answered.

Valerie straightened in her chair. "I can take care of myself. I'm not interested in taking care of anyone else."

"You take care of public relations and other situations similar to our problem with the mayor," Elisabeth said pointedly.

"I do, yes." She gestured at her clothes, then at Elisabeth's simple ponytail and outfit. "I fought politically prewar. I would prefer to keep my hands clean postwar. That is why I do what I do."

"That's kind of a ridiculous answer, don't you think?" Elisabeth blurted.

Valerie stared at Elisabeth for a beat before she finally smiled. "I like you," she declared. "Your honesty is very refreshing."

"I appreciate that," Elisabeth replied. "I do have some more questions, though."

"I'm sure they match mine."

"Can you smell the undead? Can you tell if someone's already infected?"

Valerie's nose crinkled. "Ugh, yes, I can. I hate knowing that I have a scent."

"Like fresh dirt I'm told," Elisabeth interrupted.

"Exactly like that." Valerie shook her head. "I'm glad they have deodorant, but perfume would be lovely."

"I find it interesting that you smell like a human to me."

She tilted her head thoughtfully, sniffed deeply. "Likewise. Perhaps it's Mother Nature's way of avoiding confusion."

Elisabeth nodded in agreement. "That would make sense. What about strength? Healing?"

"I don't think I could do what you did to those men last night, but they would still be dead today had that been me. The healing I have found increases in speed the more serious the wound."

Elisabeth touched her shoulder where she had been shot. The hole was gone, but it was still tender. "Are there no other Abnormals that you've met?"

Valerie cast her eyes downward. "I know they exist throughout the company. I tend to stay away from the teams."

"You don't like the violence. That's really why you aren't a team leader, isn't it?" Elisabeth asked gently.

The mouthpiece turned her hands, palms facing upward, and shrugged. "You caught me."

"You work for Zombie Response Team."

"I know in whose employ I am."

Elisabeth stopped pressing for more details. Instead, she asked, "How upset is Ethan that I killed humans?"

"They were trying to kidnap you and hurt you. I saw him watching the cleanup crew take care of your mess. I think he actually admired your work," Valerie admitted. "I would suggest that, should you find yourself in a similar situation, don't leave such a tough job for the cleaners."

"I'll keep that in mind."

"Ma'am?" Rhys popped his head in the doorway.

"It's been done."

Elisabeth's face fell. "Already?"

"I gave him the needle to use whenever he was ready after he met with his family and the lawyer today."

She wiped a tear from her eye. "I should have been able to say goodbye."

"He didn't want to say anymore goodbyes. He thanked us for giving him time to settle his affairs and tell everyone he cares about that he loves them."

"What about the body?"

"Dallas severed the brain stem. It's been moved to the funeral home. His family wants a traditional burial."

"Thank you, Rhys." Elisabeth dismissed her teammate.

After remaining silent throughout their exchange, Valerie began to speak. "You allowed an infected to do all of that? Protocol states that they be eliminated immediately."

"I will adjust protocol as I find it necessary," Elisabeth snapped. She softened. "I'm sorry, Valerie. I didn't mean to be rude."

Valerie waved her hand. "No apology necessary. I understand. I admire that you still have a heart for those poor souls who are going to turn."

Elisabeth sighed. "Every single one," she replied simply.

❖ ❖ ❖

ETHAN PACED ANXIOUSLY back and forth in Elisabeth's office, his hands clasped behind him.

Team Mayfair watched him from the breakroom. "Does he know we have a spare office just for visitors?" Rhys asked.

"Doubtful," Elisabeth grumbled. She sat at the table and took a sip of her black coffee.

Dumping a spoonful of sugar into her own cup, Amelia said, "Maybe he just likes your taste of décor."

"There's nothing in there," Dallas noted.

Amelia pointed at him and winked. "Exactly. No personal things to indicate personal space. He might just think that's the traveling office."

"She had plans to plaster the walls with photos of her and the mayor. Kissy face, kissy face." Rhys made smooching sounds.

"Rhys." Elisabeth's voice was low.

He continued. "Everything was going fine until you just had to show him up. Men like that don't like to lose against women."

Dallas choked back a laugh. "What do you know about women or relationships in general? This is coming from a person who won't take no for an answer and keeps pestering poor Tammy."

Rhys pointed to himself with both thumbs. "This guy knows a lot about relationships."

"Oh, really?" Dallas said, a brow raised skeptically.

"Oh, for goodness' sake, it's because he's actually dating Tammy," Elisabeth said. She took another gulp of her coffee, finishing it.

Rhys and Dallas blanched. Amelia just smiled.

"You knew?" Elisabeth asked Amelia.

"Sure. I saw them out a couple of times taking walks in the park by my house. I ducked out of the way before they saw me. Didn't want to seem creepy."

"You saw us?"

Amelia looked at Rhys. "You walked in the park by *my* house. What, you don't think I like to get out and enjoy that area, too?"

"Can't get any privacy around here," Rhys mumbled.

"I didn't know," Dallas said helpfully.

Rhys brightened, slapped his teammate on his back. "That's right you didn't, buddy."

Tammy entered the breakroom and poured herself a cup of coffee. Without looking up, she said, "To answer your question, Rhys, I will not go out with you. Stop even thinking about it."

Rhys grabbed Elisabeth's mug and took it to the sink next to the coffee pot.

"You better plan on washing it or sticking that in the dish washer. I've told you I'm not cleaning up your mess," Tammy warned.

Rhys grasped her shoulders and kissed her on her cheek. "Gig's up, hun."

Tammy's face burned scarlet. "Ah. Well, then." She excused herself and hurriedly left the breakroom.

"She can be really shy about personal matters," Rhys explained sheepishly.

"How long can that man pace?" Dallas asked, drawing attention back to the Division Tennessee leader.

"He'll stop when Valerie comes back from quarantine," Elisabeth answered.

"That's the real gossip of the day," Amelia said, her voice almost a whisper.

"How many more of them do you think ZRT has floating around its ranks?" Dallas asked.

"Them?" Rhys asked.

Dallas' eyes flickered to Elisabeth's. "You know what I mean."

"I don't know," Elisabeth answered honestly. "I didn't know about Valerie until this morning. From my understanding, though, she doesn't know the answer either. She tends to stay away from the teams when she's in Nashville."

"Why?" Amelia asked.

"Because when you've seen what she's seen, you'd understand."

The team turned to see Ethan standing in the doorway. He breezed past the table and opened the cabinet to pull out a mug. He filled it with water and placed it in the microwave. While waiting for the water to boil, he rummaged in another cabinet for a tea bag.

"What could she have possibly seen that we haven't?" Dallas asked. "We've all survived the war. There isn't anything you could show me that would surprise me nowadays."

The microwave beeped and Ethan carefully removed his mug, dunking the tea bag. "You need some black tea. This green tea tastes the way hay smells," he said, his nose crinkling.

The team looked at him expectedly.

"All right, fine." He sighed.

NINE

SIX YEARS AGO

Valerie Castle cast her hazel eyes upon the White House. It had been a year since the outbreak had occurred and they had all stayed for as long as they could. Staff had made it a permanent home by taking over the multiple rooms, and it wasn't uncommon to groggily pass the president in the middle of the night on the way to the restroom. She herself had always maintained an air of professionalism, something for which the president had personally thanked her. She didn't tell him that she hadn't done it for his benefit. She had done it for hers. Maintaining a sense of normalcy was the only thing that made it easier for her to get through each day.

Now she stood staring at what she considered her home, steeling herself against the sobs that threatened to wrack her body. They were moving everyone to a secure bunker where the government would, hopefully, continue to exist. If humanity survived, they would need a governing body to bring back order and justice to burgeoning communities.

She had chosen to wear a classic, elegant black pantsuit with matching pumps. She had thrown a dark pink wool coat over her shoulders to shield herself from the winter cold. She noticed a few other staff members tossing nasty glances in her direction as they moved past her in jeans, sweatshirts, and sneakers. She knew they thought she was being unreasonable and unaccepting of the circumstances, but her outfit was her coping mechanism.

"I'll see you at the bunker," the president had said. He squeezed her shoulder lightly before entering his bullet-proof vehicle. Not that he needed it; bullets were needed for zombies, not humans.

Valerie slid into the plush leather seat of a town car she shared with four other staff members. No one spoke, the mood too somber. She watched as the convoy of vehicles began to leave one by one until it was, finally, their turn. She absently noticed they were two cars behind the president as she watched the familiar landmarks of Washington D.C. slip away and fade to countryside. Her heart ached, but she held her composure.

She was certain they had reached Amish country in Pennsylvania. She envied them; they were having the easiest transition of all as electricity and water stopped running and other luxuries fell to the wayside. She and her colleagues had been lucky that the White House ran off its own generator when the power plant failed. They knew it was the beginning of the end and filled their gas tanks, packed necessary belongings, and were forced to leave her beloved city.

Farther north, snow blanketed the fields and road. It was almost blinding with the sun bouncing off the bright, white snow and Valerie was glad she wasn't the one driving yet. There was a tree line ahead and she watched it approaching quickly, hoping the overhanging branches would block out some of the overpowering light so the drivers would be able to see more easily.

Up ahead, the first car suddenly disappeared into a large, gaping hole that the snow had been covering. The other vehicles immediately slammed on their brakes. "Don't hit the brakes!" she yelled to her driver. "Drive around!"

Panicked, the driver didn't listen and the town car lurched forward, then began to slide. "Cut the gas and steer into the slide!" she shouted. This time, the driver listened and the car came to a halt.

She and the other occupants fled out of the car to help the others. The rest of the vehicles had smashed into each other's rears and her first thought was the president. Seeing so many people crowding his car, she ran past it and to the hole where the first vehicle had disappeared.

It had crumpled like a soda can and she could see blood smeared on the windows. Determined, she called, "Is anyone okay? We're here. We can help you!"

Silence.

Jerry Paltrow, the speech writer, was already in motion, tying an end of a rope around his waist. He tied the opposite end around a nearby boulder and began to climb backward into the hole. He landed on top of the trunk and shouted for someone to get him a crowbar.

Alan Smith, a secret service agent, found one in the back of another trunk, and tossed it to Jerry. Jerry pried open the trunk. "The back seats lie down and I can crawl through the trunk to get to the interior," he explained.

He was soon out of sight, but Valerie could hear him grunting with effort as he tried to kick forward a seat that still held an occupant. She swallowed the hysteria that was rising.

"I've got one!" he shouted excitedly. Alan motioned for other people to help pull Jerry and the survivor out of the hole.

The rope burned her hands as she pulled, but Valerie ignored the pain. Jerry had his arms wrapped tightly around Genevieve Lars, the Secretary of State. Half of her face was covered in blood and was already bruising from the impact.

"Almost there!" Alan shouted as he tugged.

An arrow flew from the sky and straight into Genevieve's chest. She went limp immediately. Jerry released her. "Get me up!" he cried.

He barely finished his sentence before an arrow pierced his heart.

"GET BACK INTO the cars!" Alan ordered, his voice booming.

Valerie rushed back to her own vehicle, arrows flying overhead. She screamed as people collapsed around her. She held the door open for Alan as he followed closely behind, but a hatchet hurled through the air and buried itself in the back of his skull.

"Shut the damn door!" barked the Secretary of Defense. Valerie pushed Alan out of the way, her hands becoming coated in his blood. She slammed the door shut and locked them all before hunkering down below the window so that she couldn't be seen.

"Get down!" she ordered the secretary. When he didn't comply, she looked at him to instruct him again. He was clutching his chest, his breathing hard. *Jesus, he's having a heart attack!* Valerie thought.

"Help me!" he begged.

Valerie was completely helpless. She grasped his hand and watched him die, grateful that it was a swift death by nature and not on the terms of whoever was attacking them. A grotesque idea popped in her head and she went with it, desperate. She still had Alan's blood on her hands and she smeared it on the side of the secretary's head, making it look like he had hit the window and it had caused hemorrhaging. She removed her dark pink coat and threw it in the front foot well. She dragged his body so that it was on top of hers, with her flattening herself on the floorboards. She hoped no one could see her lying underneath his body.

The screaming stopped and she began to hear unfamiliar voices.

"We're going to feast tonight!" she heard a deep voice say.

Her stomach lurched as she drew the horrifying conclusion.

"You and you, take the dead and start the preparations. You three, round up the rest and put them in the cage. We'll keep them fresh," said another male voice.

One of the staff members began to argue. She couldn't tell who it was, but a scream followed. The leader shouted, "I know who all of you are. Does anyone else want to tell me that we can't do what we're doing? Does anyone else want to tell me that what we're doing is wrong? We're in a war, kids. We're doing everything we can to survive while you assholes live up life in your swanky White House, and now your swanky cars, off to some swanky place upstate to live out the rest of this war we're fighting for you. Let me tell you something, kids! This was not our intention, but meat is meat!"

Valerie began to shudder uncontrollably with fear.

Heavy footsteps neared her car and she heard the handles of each door begin to jiggle. "It's locked!"

"How many are in there?" the leader asked.

Valerie stopped breathing to remain perfectly still.

"Some old guy," came the response.

"How much?"

A pause. "Eh. He's not worth it to try and bust out bullet-proof glass. Skin and bones, mostly."

"Leave him, then," the leader instructed.

Hearing the footsteps grow fainter, Valerie let out a gasp of air. She didn't dare leave her position as she listened for the attackers to leave. She waited for what she felt was an hour, then slowly moved to check the wrist of the Secretary of Defense for a watch. He was wearing an expense platinum Rolex, and she apologized as she removed it and slid it onto her own wrist.

The sun began to drop until it disappeared completely and Valerie started to lose feeling in her hands and feet. If she didn't do something, she was going to freeze to death. She risked rolling the secretary's body onto the back seat and peered through the window. She watched carefully, her eyes like a hawk. Satisfied that no one was out there, she manually unlocked a back door to reduce noise.

She quickly checked the other vehicles for survivors and found no one, not even the dead. By the road, she spotted sled marks leading off to what she assumed was the tree line. It was too dark to see, but she knew her pumps were creating too much racket, and she reluctantly removed them. The snow-covered road soaked through her stocking feet, and she knew she needed to remedy her problem immediately. She roamed from car to car, checking bags until she found Lauren Wilder's suitcase. She was an aide and close to Valerie's size.

Valerie pulled the bag into another vehicle with her and locked the doors. Staying as low as she could, she changed out of her suit and into dark jeans and a navy-blue wool sweater. She also found sweatpants and pulled them over her jeans for extra warmth. She layered her feet in several pairs of socks before putting on a pair of sneakers. She was grateful that Lauren's feet were a size bigger to accommodate the extra padding. "Lauren, if you're alive, I owe you," she whispered to herself.

The noise of a car door opening made Valerie's blood run cold. She looked out of the back window and saw someone in the car she had occupied earlier. The person dragged out the secretary's body and began to pound his head against the pavement, his skull finally cracking to spill its contents which the person scooped into his mouth greedily.

Valerie ducked down and weighed her options. Intelligence reports had stated that older zombies could figure out small things like opening doors or windows. Unfortunately, she wasn't sure if this was a zombie or one of the crazed, cannibalistic humans she had encountered earlier. It was too dark to make out anything other than a male outline.

The person finished its meal and stood up, shuffling her way. It was fight or flight, and Valerie decided she'd been through too much hell already to give up. She opened the console and found what she was looking for: a bright orange rescue safety hammer. While their original use is to smash windows or cut seat belts in case of emergencies, Valerie had another idea.

Quietly, she exited the car and was careful to not shut the door back all of the way. She wanted it to look closed, but didn't want to make a sound. She hunched over to make her body smaller as she slowly circled her uninvited guest.

He stopped and began moving toward her. Relief flooded through her. A zombie, she assumed, was easier to kill than a human. Valerie herself hadn't killed any undead yet, and she tried to swallow her nervousness. She raised the hammer and ran forward. She brought it down with all of her might, yet barely grazed the side of its head.

She raised her arm to swing again and the zombie lunged, sinking his teeth into the flesh on her opposite shoulder. She cried out in pain and began striking the zombie as hard as she could with the hammer. It fell to her feet and she kept hitting it until its skull caved.

Valerie's shoulder throbbed and she went back to the car where she'd gotten the hammer and searched frantically for a first aid kit. Finding one, she locked herself inside and painfully removed the sweater to attend to her wound. She mopped off the blood that ran down her arm and wiped disinfectant, followed by antibiotic ointment, over the wound. Taping a large bandage over it, she pulled the sweater back over her head. She already knew she was a dead woman. She had heard of bite survivors, but dismissed them as a myth.

Looking at her newly acquired watch, she noted the date and time. She had one week left.

She didn't fight back the tears as they rushed over her cheeks. She finally let go of her composure she had so strongly grasped and cried until she fell asleep.

SIX DAYS PASSED and Valerie had seen no one. She had searched each car for a weapon and found none that would quickly end her life. The secret service had guns and they were gone, along with the people who had carried them. She thought she would die of dehydration, but couldn't bring herself to cause such an awful death. Instead, she ate the snow for its moisture and munched on a bag of peanuts that she found stashed in Jerry's bag. How he had managed to find them and keep them hidden was a marvel to her, but she was grateful for his sneakiness.

She gave up trying to clean her shoulder. She didn't want to waste precious supplies on herself when she knew that, should someone else come along, they could find the kit and use it.

That night, she looked at her watch and sighed. She thought about her parents who had died when she was young from a car accident. They had become another drunken driver statistic and her grandparents took her into their home. They were wonderful people and she had deeply mourned their deaths. Her grandfather died from pneumonia, her grandmother following a few days later. Valerie knew it was from a broken heart. They had been so incredibly in love and she had hoped she would find that for herself one day. She had had a dual funeral for them, whispering her goodbyes as she stood between their caskets at the grave site.

She had finished school, walking across the stage to accept her law degree and wishing she still had family left to share her special moment. She went out with friends and got too drunk on red wine, taking a cab home when she was too wobbly to even walk.

Valerie had been working her way up at a prestigious law firm when one of the partners, William O'Connor, ran and won the presidency. He had appointed her his chief of staff and she happily accepted. With no one at home waiting for her, she was able to dedicate her entire life to the president.

Her life had been a good one despite the losses she had suffered.

Locking herself in one of the scattered vehicles, she buckled her seat belt. She hoped that, when she turned, she'd be unable to escape the confines of the car and hurt people. If she was lucky, someone would come along, find her, and put her out of her undead misery.

She began to shiver from the cold and reached into the suitcase beside her. *No sense in freezing before I die*, she thought. She layered more sweaters over her and used a coat as a blanket. She leaned her head against the headrest and closed her eyes, willing sleep to come quickly.

The next morning, her eyes flew open. She took in her surroundings and saw that the snow was finally receding.

Wait, did I get my days confused? Valerie checked the expensive time piece, brought it up to her ear to make sure it was still ticking. It had been seven days since she'd been bitten, yet here she sat, alive and well. She pulled her sweaters away from her shoulder and could only see a fading bruise. Frowning, she hopped in the front seat and pulled down the visor. She pushed her shoulder close to the vanity mirror and gingerly touched the area where she had been bitten. The punctures from the zombie's teeth were gone, an ugly yellow ring in its place. She let go of the sweaters and they snapped back into place.

As she flipped the visor back in place, she caught her face in the mirror. The irises had turned crimson. She stared at her reflection, blinking several times in disbelief.

She drummed her fingers against the console, thinking. Were she to get wounded again, it was going to heal. She could face other zombies without fearing the bite. More importantly, she could face other humans and not fear their weapons. "Unless it's a hatchet to the back of my head," she muttered to herself.

She got out of the car and began walking, stopping at the hole that had swallowed the first car a week prior. She stared at the crumpled vehicle curiously and jumped in, landing on top of the trunk with a loud thud. She wanted to test herself, see what else came along with the bite other than the weird eye color. She also knew that Genevieve owed her plump figure to the snacks she always carried, and Valerie hoped there were some left that she could take. She was absolutely starving after living for seven days on snow alone.

The trunk was still open and she found the crowbar Jerry had used. Inside were two suitcases, and Valerie chose the closest one. Disappointed to find more clothing that she didn't need, she yanked out the second suitcase. Her eyes widened with surprise: it was filled with nothing but food. She ripped open various packages and ate hungrily. She stuffed the few cans Genevieve had packed into her coat pockets, hoping to find a can opener later.

She took the crowbar and tossed it to the top of the hole. She found the straggly end of the rope the cannibals had cut to remove Jerry and used it to climb out, surprised at how easy it was for her. Reaching down to retrieve the crowbar, she heard several footsteps and snapped back up, holding the piece of metal like a bat. She could see zombies coming her way and she was ready to defend herself.

They passed her, never even noticing her existence.

Valerie laughed manically. She felt great. Invincible. She turned toward the tree line and narrowed her eyes.

NO SNOW HAD fallen in the last week, and the tracks left by the cannibals' sled were still visible. Free from the threat of zombie attacks, Valerie was able to peruse the various luggage for more supplies without worrying about watching her surroundings or straining to hear shuffling feet. She found the can opener in Genevieve's purse and put everything into a backpack. She happily discovered a couple of plastic bags and tied them around her feet to keep her sneakers from getting wet and set out on her journey.

Bundled against the cold, Valerie picked up the sled tracks and began to follow them. The snow crunched beneath her feet and she was glad she had found protective coverings to help keep her feet a little warmer. When she reached the tree line, she realized the forest that it led to was thicker than she had assumed. She continued following the tracks, sometimes having to double back when she lost them under bare spots in the snow where it couldn't penetrate the canopy of limbs and evergreens. She noticed footprints as well, hoping to use those in case she lost the sled tracks again.

Night began to fall and Valerie was ravenous. She gathered branches that she hoped weren't too wet to burn and sighed with relief when the tiny flame from her stolen lighter began to lick the base of the wood. She opened a can of chicken noodle soup and held it over the fire with two sticks. When it was cooked, she ate it slowly and felt the warmth spread from her belly to the rest of her body. The soup was gone too quickly, but she didn't dare eat more. She didn't know how long it would be until she found more food.

She eyed the trees around her and found a spot. Reluctantly, she kicked snow on her fire until the flames were gone and climbed up a tree. With her condition, it was an easy task, and she made sure she was out of sight should any human pass her. She wished she had rope to tie herself to the limb so she wouldn't fall out in the middle of the night, but she had left that behind, never thinking she would need it.

Valerie woke the next morning shivering. She didn't know if she could die from hypothermia now, but she wasn't willing to risk her life to answer the question. She stretched as well as she could from her position and stood up slowly, balancing herself carefully on the limb that had been her bed. She looked up and began to climb, her arms and legs gaining more feeling as she moved.

She stopped when she reached the last branch that would hold her weight and looked out as far as she could see. There was a ring of smoke that looked like it was coming from chimneys and she climbed down the tree, grabbing her backpack along the way.

Feet on the ground, she stretched once more and began walking at a brisk pace. She snacked on stale coffeecake and silently thanked the dead Secretary of State for her meal. The sun was slowly moving across the sky, its pale-yellow light shining beautifully against the snow. Valerie almost felt like she could have been on a casual walk in the woods, enjoying a rare day off before returning to the hustle and bustle of the White House.

She could smell the smoke she had seen that morning and checked her watch. She'd been trekking for almost ninety minutes. The trees began to thin out around her and she slowed her pace, moving from tree to tree, trying to gauge her surroundings.

It was a spacious clearing filled with several cabins that had once been used for vacationers. Each cabin style was different, though they all had a large front porch and green tin roofs. There were trails that led out into the woods with markings still visible for hikers. There was a central cabin that was bigger than the others, a lodge used for group gatherings and housing the main office where visitors would check in for their week away from the real world. Valerie spotted a road leading into the little village and surmised it must lead back to the main highway. Her group would have passed it on their way up-state had they not been ambushed.

A familiar cologne entered her nostrils and she inhaled deeply. It was faint and mingled with something else. *Decay.* Like an animal, Valerie followed the scent and covered her mouth to stop the scream trying to escape her lips.

It was a body hanging upside down, the throat slit. Its blood had drained and was frozen on the forest floor. Valerie looked closer and horror mounted inside her. She did not want this body to belong to the president. The face was distorted and purple, but Valerie could tell by the *Notre Dame* sweatshirt that it was the vice president. A tear slid down her cheek and she wiped it away. He had been a good man. "I promise you'll see a proper burial, sir," she whispered.

She hid behind the trees and waited patiently. Hours passed and the sun began to sink below the horizon. Finally, she saw people exiting the cabins and going to the central lodge. They were carrying small tools that they could stick in their back pockets, and Valerie decided they were for potential attacks along the trail. No one spoke. They simply walked single-file until they disappeared behind the heavy doors of what Valerie dubbed The Lodge. There had to be a dining hall where they all ate together.

She didn't see anyone leave the smallest cabin on the farthest edge of the community, and she used the darkness to conceal her as she ran across the clearing to it. There was a lock on the door that broke when she gently tugged it. Immediately she began hearing sobs, and she entered the cabin cautiously.

"Please, you just took Ronald!" cried a female voice.

"Hush!" Valerie said. "I'm not here to hurt you. I'm Valerie Castle."

An excited murmur ran through the group. "Valerie!" exclaimed a deep male voice. "Thank God! We thought you were dead."

"Not yet, Mr. President," Valerie responded. "How many of you are left?"

"Twelve," he replied.

Valerie's heart sank. "Only twelve? What about the others?"

"They're not just feeding themselves. It's like it's the nineteenth century here. They have cows, dogs, pigs, chickens, and maybe others I didn't see on our way in," President William O'Connor answered.

Valerie shook her head sadly. She hadn't seen any of that, but she hadn't gone around to the back of the cabins either. "Do they keep a weapons stash here?"

"They took all of ours. I'm not sure where they are, but a good guess would be that main building they all seem to use."

"All right. Give me thirty minutes and I'll be back," Valerie promised.

"Absolutely not. One of us is going with you."

"No. Stay here," she ordered. She left the cabin and ripped off the plastic bags that had been covering her sneakers. They were going to be too loud for what she had planned.

VALERIE SNUCK AROUND to the back of the cabins and saw the barn and various farm animals the president had mentioned. While he had a good suggestion that the weapons would be stored at The Lodge, Valerie disagreed with him. The leader would want all of the good stuff for himself and guessed the biggest cabin would belong to him. She smashed the backdoor window with a stick, reached in, and unlocked it. The hinges creaked as she opened the door and she didn't bother closing it behind her. She searched the rooms until she found what she was looking for: a bookshelf converted into a makeshift gun rack. She found the Glocks that belonged to the White House secret service and checked their magazines. They were still full, having not had a chance to fire when they had been attacked. She put a few into her backpack and stuffed two more into the back of her jeans. She wasn't familiar with guns and chose a rifle with a decent-looking scope to take as well.

She crept back down the stairs and out the door, not daring to touch it for fear the sound might be heard. She dashed back to the survivors, identifying herself once again.

"I need the best shooter you've got," she said.

"That would be me," said the president, stepping forward.

"I need the best shooter you've got that isn't the President of the United States," Valerie clarified.

"I'm not going to argue with you, Valerie. I'm the best one here."

"Sir, we're going to get out of here. We're going to go back to the cars and we're going to continue to our destination. This country still needs its president and that man is you."

"We can't risk going to the cars. That's too much ground in the open," he argued.

"We'll be fine. Please trust me."

"I'm going to help you," the president insisted.

"Fine." Valerie was tired of wasting time. "Everyone else, you're going to stay here and you're going to block that door and wait for us." She passed out the guns she had taken except for one she kept for herself and the rifle. "Let's go, Mr. President."

Valerie led the president to a tree facing The Lodge. "If you climb this, can you shoot whatever comes out?" she asked.

"Yes," he answered, determined. He looked at the tree and frowned. "I don't think I can reach the lowest limb."

"Not an issue." Valerie clasped her hands together to create a stair. "I'll boost you up, sir."

The president looked at her incredulously. "We need to find another tree I can reach."

Valerie yanked the collar of her sweater to the side to reveal a fading bruise. "I got bitten. I survived. I'm an Abnormal. I have some more special traits now, one of them being strength. Stop second-guessing me. You wouldn't if we were back on Pennsylvania Avenue."

Stunned, the president stepped backward. "I don't know what to say."

"Say nothing to the others. Now get up that tree!" She re-clasped her hands and launched him upward. He grabbed the lowest branch and hauled himself upward, then lay down on his chest, resting the butt of the rifle against his shoulder. He looked through the scope and swore to himself.

Valerie left him and approached The Lodge slowly. She kept herself hunched over until she reached the front porch. Using the porch to block her body, she snuck a glance through the front window and saw what the president had seen: a buffet. The body supplying that night's dinner was off to the side, set up like a carving station. She vomited involuntarily and absently wiped her mouth. The world was probably going to end, but no one should ever resort to cannibalism.

She removed her lighter from her pocket and lit the edge of the porch. It took less time than she had expected to catch fire and she quietly rounded the cabin setting more spots aflame. She made sure to light the back windows and doors to prevent any surprises and returned to the front where she waited.

Smoke filled the interior and the screams began. "Out the front! Out the front! The back is blocked!"

The occupants burst through the door and Valerie started shooting. She wasn't very accurate; she had wanted to hit their heads. Instead, she hit necks, shoulders, and stomachs. They still went down, so she wasn't as concerned with them. She would finish them later.

She was soon out of bullets and President O'Connor took over, firing true shots to their heads. Under his cover, she removed some of the tools she had seen from their back pockets, finding a hammer and a long screwdriver.

The president ran out of ammunition and Valerie found the few that were left, ending them with swift, merciful blows to their skulls. She checked the ones she had merely wounded and killed them quickly until she found who she was looking for: the leader.

She had caught him in his stomach, the blood almost black as it spilled through the fingers he desperately used to staunch the bleeding. She crouched down next to him.

"Who are you?" he demanded, his voice weakening.

She ignored his question. "You're an evil person."

"We do what we have to so that we can survive," he seethed.

"You can survive and not taste human flesh."

"We'd be dead by now if we had already killed our livestock. You must supplement the diet."

Valerie thought of the staff, the people she had grown to admire and care for over time. She whipped out the screwdriver, placed it on the leader's head, and began to hammer.

She was not merciful. She took her time.

VALERIE HELPED THE president down from the tree and joined the other survivors. They checked the remaining cabin for others and found no one; she and the president had killed them all.

They stayed for the rest of the night, eating the food that Valerie had scavenged. The next morning, they took turns digging a grave for the vice president, doing the best that they could to honor his memory.

Using the road to get back to the cars instead of going through the forest, they were able to reach them within a day. She dug out her black suit and changed out of her blood-splattered clothes.

They piled into three vehicles and continued their trip, Valerie in the lead.

TEN

Everyone was quiet after Ethan Brown finished his story. Rhys broke the silence. "She's got two up on me. I haven't seen cannibals and I certainly haven't saved the president."

"We voted him back in. Why did she leave him?" Amelia asked. "Seems like a flashy job."

"She had been doing that job for far longer than the eight years max she had expected, thanks to the war. She was tired," Ethan said simply.

Noticing Valerie approaching from the hallway, Elisabeth straightened. "Did he tell you anything?" she asked.

"Your mayor has quite the mouth on him when he's angry. He's not willing to discuss the research laboratory with us. He wants some assurances first. I have informed him that he will be unable to remain in his current position as we have already issued a statement, however, I could find him a job more suitable to his skills."

"Tell him whatever he needs to hear," Ethan ordered.

"One of the assurances he wants is that we won't kill him," Valerie said, her red eyes meeting Ethan's. "I've already told him that we don't operate in that manner," she added coolly. "We're not the government."

Elisabeth stifled a laugh.

"Go back down and talk to him. Elisabeth, go with her, please."

Valerie followed Elisabeth back down the stairs, her heels echoing in the hallway. Todd Wilkins was sitting smugly in his chair, his arms crossed. He didn't bother to stand as they entered his cell.

"Bringing her here isn't going to change anything," he said.

"I doubt that," Valerie responded easily. She casually leaned against the wall. "I notice your roommate is gone."

Todd craned his neck to see behind him. "He's dead."

"No, he's not," Elisabeth lied.

Todd narrowed his eyes. "He was infected. I saw all of those people go to see him and say their farewells."

"What you saw was a charade. His family believes he was infected. The truth is that he's like our friend here," Valerie said, gesturing to Elisabeth.

"And you," Todd clarified. "I'm not an idiot."

"Yes, yes, like me as well," Valerie replied dismissively. "You see, Mr. Wilkins, the ZRT has its own labs where research is conducted ethically. People like myself volunteer under safe conditions where no harm will become them. To ensure these volunteers keep approaching us, we need to keep them from wanting to hide. Your methods will encourage that, and that I cannot allow."

"My methods are effective. They might not be as *ethical* as yours, but we will get results," he argued.

"Am I to assume from that statement that you have found no Abnormals to test?" Valerie asked, an eyebrow raised.

Todd spat at Elisabeth's feet. "I found one. I underestimated the difficulty it would be to bring her in."

"That behavior is unnecessary," Valerie murmured. She paced the room, her hands on her hips. "We want to know where your lab is. Your scientists will be integrated with ours because brilliant minds cannot be wasted, though they will be briefed on appropriate protocols with our test subjects. We want to know who your partner is because I can assure you that if you don't answer that question, you will regret it. Once you have helped us, we will help you. We will move you wherever you want and take care of your needs for up to one year.

That is the final offer you will receive. There will be absolutely no ne-gotiations." Valerie stopping pacing and stared directly at Todd.

He flinched reflexively under her fierce gaze. He uncrossed his arms but remained seated. Several moments passed as he weighed his options. Finally, he spoke: "The lab is on the outskirts of Zone Four."

"And your partner?" Valerie prompted.

"Come back with a better offer and I'll tell you."

"Are you sure that is how you want to respond?"

Todd smirked. "There are always other options."

"Yes, of course, Mr. Wilkins." Valerie drew a fingernail across her palm, her bright red blood materializing in its wake. In an instant, she was behind the former mayor, her hand over his mouth.

Todd's cries were muffled as he tried to keep his mouth closed. Valerie placed her thumb over his chin and pulled, then smeared her blood across his lips. She released him and wiped the rest of her blood on his blanket, the wound on her hand already sealing itself.

Todd frantically wiped at his face, trying to remove the red sub-stance. "You bitch!" he shouted.

"I told you there was no need for that behavior. I also told you that there were absolutely no negotiations."

Elisabeth could already smell the infection spreading.

"I don't sense an infection yet," Valerie lied. "That means you might become like one of us, which will make you far more useful and valuable. Your value, however, is only guided by your cooperation. You have twelve hours."

The cell door locked automatically behind them as they left. Elisabeth was quiet until she was sure that Todd could not hear them. "Why did you infect him?"

"The partner might be false. He's most likely acting alone and is using the possible fictional character as bait so that we won't kill him. The lab, on the other hand, is real and would have been difficult to locate. I have no doubt we would have found it, but his cooperation makes that detail easier. Giving him the hope that he could become like us and, therefore, more valuable, is simply a tactical move. Now his final acts are more of a chance for him to redeem his character." Valerie glanced at Elisabeth out of the corner of her eye. "It might make you feel less guilty for dating him if he comes through for us."

"I doubt that."

Valerie stopped and looked at Elisabeth directly. She patted her arm and said, "We all make mistakes. Some more than others."

"HONEY, I'M SO glad that you came for dinner." Ruth Mayfair smiled warmly at her daughter.

"Of course, Mom. It was delicious." Elisabeth stood and collected her mother and sister's plates.

Ruth put her hand over her daughter's. "I'll take care of this. I know you've had a hard day."

"Thanks," Elisabeth replied.

With their mother out of the room, Margo asked, "What's wrong with you?"

"Nothing. Just another hectic day at the office."

Margo nodded, skeptical. "Uh-huh. Listen, I heard about the mayor. I'm really sorry."

Elisabeth stifled her laughter. "That relationship was never going to go beyond the second date." She explained what had happened at the gym.

"I told you I didn't have a good feeling about him." Margo paused, and tilted her head thoughtfully. "You're not telling me everything. You wouldn't have ditched him just because he was a sore loser."

"He saw me."

Margo's eyes narrowed and she leaned forward. "He saw you fighting against the zombies? My stars, Elisabeth, what in the hell were you thinking?" Margo's voice was rising.

"I was thinking that there were a lot of zombies and a lot of innocent people that I needed to save. I thought he was outside with Rhys and the others," Elisabeth replied defensively.

"Damn it, Elisabeth. You have to be more careful!" Margo's hands were clenched into fists, her mouth a straight line.

"Calm down!" Elisabeth said softly. "I don't want Mom to worry. Besides, he's not able to tell anyone anything now."

Margo leaned forward and lowered her voice. "Because he's dead," she stated bluntly.

Elisabeth shook her head. "No, he's not dead. Not yet, anyway."

"I thought you killed the infected immediately?" Margo leaned back in her chair and crossed her arms.

"Not always right away. We let the gym coach get his affairs in order and say goodbye before we euthanized him," Elisabeth explained.

Margo's face brightened. "Oh, what a great story that would be! That would help the community feel better should they happened to get bitten. 'Zombie Response Team: Humanitarians.'" She scrunched her face. "The name could use some work."

"No, no stories. He was a special case."

"Oh," Margo replied, disappointed. Noticing her sister's expression, she added, "I'm sorry. He really must have been special if you let him live that long."

"He was. He was trying to share his knowledge and build confidence in people." Elisabeth felt her throat tighten. "I hate that this damn war isn't over, that people are still getting infected. We've got hordes showing up at random places that turns out aren't so random after all. We've got testing being done and secret labs…" Elisabeth trailed off, struggling to regain her composure.

Margo hugged her twin sister and rocked her back and forth gently.

Like a dam, a flood of angry tears burst and ran down Elisabeth's cheeks. "I can't stop them. I don't know how. The company has a theory, but I think it's them grasping at straws because they don't know either." She stopped, wiped her eyes, and blew her nose. "I'm sorry. Again."

Margo leaned back into her chair. "It's okay. You're so strong, but you don't have to be with me. I love you even when you have an ugly cry." She smiled.

Elisabeth chuckled quietly. Her sister always knew how to make her laugh at even her darkest moments.

"What do you mean hordes and labs?" Margo asked curiously. "Off the record," she clarified.

Elisabeth hesitated and was silent for a few moments. "There was the horde at the park by Amelia's and then another at the gym. We found an outbuilding filled with more zombies. They had to have been poor souls that remained outside of the safe zones. I understand a few getting infected and turning, but it's clear that someone has been taking them, turning them, and releasing them in areas where they can access the public. For what purpose, we don't know. The ZRT thinks someone knows about their plans to downsize the amount of actual response teams and focus more on the labs they have."

"They have labs?" Margo shook her head angrily. "I told you they would have labs! I warned you that they would want to come after you and others like you for testing."

"No, you misunderstand. They only want volunteers," Elisabeth explained, trying to calm her sister.

"For now," Margo said, seething.

"Look, they're better than the secret lab we found. Team Churchill is handling it now and it will be dismantled by sunrise."

"Tell me about this secret lab." When Elisabeth didn't respond, Margo said, "That's why Todd is still alive, isn't it? He's the one who was running it. He's not even infected, is he? How did you find out?"

"He actually is infected," Elisabeth admitted.

"Why did you do that?" Margo demanded.

"I didn't do it. Ethan's mouthpiece did. She's like me. She called his bluff and we're waiting to see how he responds. He doesn't know he's infected."

"What did you learn?" Margo asked again.

"He didn't even have any test subjects. He tried." Elisabeth's face was grim. "He was unsuccessful. We're absorbing his scientists into our own research facilities."

"Then why bother messing with him further? What else does he have to offer?" Margo pressed.

"I think he has a partner."

A shadow briefly crossed Margo's face, so subtle Elisabeth almost didn't notice it. "What does everyone else think?"

"They think it's a bluff so that we'll keep him around longer," Elisabeth answered.

"How long does he have until you decide to let him go? Surely you aren't going to allow him to turn."

Elisabeth frowned. "We have one week. We're at the mercy of time now. I hope I'm wrong about the partner."

"Have they asked you to volunteer yet for testing?" Margo asked, timid.

"No, of course not. They're not going to force anyone," Elisabeth said reassuringly. "They would only ask if they didn't have enough, and they know I'm too busy anyway."

Margo said nothing, her thoughts racing. She remained quiet, even as their mother rejoined them, chattering happily about the Scrabble tournament that she had entered. Ruth remained oblivious to her daughter's discontent, nodding only in response when Margo excused herself to go to sleep early.

"YOU'RE MY ITTY-BITTY sweetheart. I love you so much, honey!" Rhys nuzzled the back of Tammy's neck.

Dallas groaned. "That's disgusting. I liked it better when you two pretended she wasn't even interested."

Tammy wrapped her arm around Rhys' back. "What can I say? We like to role play."

"I *will* puke. I promise you that," Dallas warned.

"Okay, we'll stop." She smacked Rhys playfully on his behind. "See you later, Tiger."

"It's going on your keyboard, in between the individual keys so that it's harder to clean. When Christmas gets here, you're going to get dried vomit in your stocking," Dallas promised.

"I got a rock in my stocking one year. It was meant to make it look full until my parents filled it with the actual gifts, but they forgot. I thought they were trying something retro, and I painted it to be my Pet Rock." Amelia grinned at the memory.

"Let's not talk about Christmas yet. It's October and Tammy's already asking me what I want. I don't even want to think about that holiday yet. I want to make it through Halloween, stuff my face at Thanksgiving, and do what every man does at Christmas," Rhys said.

"What does every man do at Christmas?" Amelia asked.

"Shop three days before," Dallas and Rhys replied in unison.

"Is that why you got me a mini muffin tin last year?"

"Don't forget the silicon baking mat," Rhys said. "It was a two for one sale."

"I don't even bake!" Amelia exclaimed.

"Well, you should start. You have a baking mat and a muffin tin. I can buy you the ingredients this year and you can bring delicious muffins for New Year's." Rhys looked at Dallas. "Dallas, wouldn't you like some baked goods?"

Dallas was reading an email. "Not from Amelia," he muttered. He looked at her apologetically. "You're welcome to stop by an actual bakery. Dad loves those bear claws." He pointed to his message. "We're all copied on this message from Ethan. He wants our team to sweep the South section."

"He also wants us to update the map of that area while we're out there," Amelia said, leaning over Dallas' shoulder. She straightened. "I'll do it. I've had experience painting rocks. That would make me the most artistic." She chuckled to herself.

The team suited up in their armor and Dallas gently knocked on Elisabeth's office door. "Come in," she invited. She didn't bother looking at them. Instead, her eyes were glued to a monitor.

"How long have you been watching him?" Dallas asked. He watched the former mayor walk the length of his cell, hands clasped behind his back. His lips were moving.

"He's talking to himself," Elisabeth said.

"Can you hear him?"

"No, we don't have audio. It's malfunctioning, but IT is working on it."

"How long are you going to wait to tell him he's infected and not an Abnormal?" Dallas prodded.

Elisabeth's eyes flashed. "Whenever Ethan gives me the green light." She noticed his armor. "Let me change and we'll go."

Ten minutes later, Dallas was driving. He annoyingly glanced at Rhys whose feet were propped on top of the dashboard.

"How did it go with Team Churchill last night?" Amelia asked. "I saw them on my way in this morning, but they looked too exhausted to talk."

"Todd failed to mention the armed guards he had. One of Nicholas' men took a hit that didn't penetrate his armor, but it did knock him down. Nicholas shot the man and the others gave up easily after that. They found the researchers inside," Elisabeth explained.

"Why were they even there if there was no one to test?" Rhys questioned.

"They had animals," Dallas answered quietly.

"Yes, they did," Elisabeth confirmed. "They've been released." She watched Dallas exhale slowly.

"Are they going to comply with our standards in our own labs?" he asked.

"Yes." Elisabeth didn't mention that two of them had been happy to cooperate. The third man screamed that science couldn't have ethics and still be progressive. He had run toward Nicholas with a broken beaker and Nicholas shot him, too.

Dallas pulled onto a road and passed a middle school and a high school. Windows were broken and weeds were growing up the sides as if pulling the buildings back into nature. They cleared the buildings quickly and continued down the road.

Amelia looked at her map. "There should be a subdivision up here."

A sign that read *Quail Hollow* was barely visible, but the road twisting downward was still in good shape. They turned right and the road branched off in two directions. They chose another right and saw a grouping of condominiums, huddled in a semicircle like Western pioneers and their wagons. They split into teams of two and began their search, finding nothing.

Rhys whistled when they regrouped. "This was one fancy neighborhood. These condos are bigger than my house was when I was growing up. This place has a pool and tennis courts. They need some TLC, but I can see why the director wants this area cleared."

"We haven't even seen the houses yet," Dallas added.

Returning to the main road of the subdivision, they went from house to house. They found the same scenario in each home: drawers opened as people had thrown clothes into suitcases, bare spots on walls as families had taken their most precious photos, and food that had been rotten for so long that it didn't smell anymore. The abodes felt almost like a tomb and the team remained silent as they walked through each room, their hearts heavy and wondering what had become of the occupants.

The road branched off once more, though they only found land with faded "For Sale" signs. "This would have been perfect for a family," Amelia murmured. She inked in a thin line on the map and simply wrote *for possible future use* where the plots were.

They approached the end of the subdivision. A large, blue house with old-fashioned white columns dotting its front porch loomed over the other homes from the hill on which it sat. The pavement on the driveway was separated into chunks, but they spotted tire tracks in the tall grass and followed them up to the garage.

"Should tracks look that fresh?" Rhys asked.

"No," Dallas answered. "Looks like we've got a squatter. Not a bad choice if I decided I didn't want to live in town."

They approached the front door and were not surprised when they found it locked. Not wanting to destroy the door on a home that someone might still occupy, Elisabeth scurried up one of the columns. She checked the windows and reluctantly broke a pane to unlock it from the inside. She pulled it open and entered the home, smelling the undead immediately. "We've got one," she whispered into her throat mic. "I'll handle it."

She checked upstairs and, finding nothing, went down the stairs. The home had been beautiful, decorated in French Country style. She walked down a hallway, looking at the photos of the family that once dwelled there. They were all smiling, so happy.

There was a basement door that led off the kitchen and she turned the knob knowing that was where her zombie would be.

Only this zombie was chained to a support beam with a dog food bowl in front of it filled with scraps of meat. It was sitting on the ground munching on what Elisabeth could only guess had been a thigh muscle. It ignored her presence and she raised her gun to put it out of its misery.

"Don't!"

Elisabeth whirled on her heel toward the voice. A tall man with flaming red hair and eyes to match stepped out from underneath the stairs. His hair was neatly combed, his beard only a few days old. He wore a blue buttoned shirt tucked into dark jeans and cognac boots. "Who are you?" she demanded.

The man chuckled. "You know me."

Elisabeth looked at him more closely and shook her head. "I don't."

"No?" He cleared his throat. "I see, then." He stuck out his hand. "I'm Heinrich Denis," he introduced himself, his voice carrying a touch of a German accent.

Elisabeth ignored his proffered hand and he awkwardly stuffed it into his pocket. "What are you doing here?"

"This is my home. Where else would I be?" he replied.

She pointed at the zombie. "What about it?"

The stranger frowned. "*It* happens to be my brother, Marcus."

"Heinrich, this is beyond inappropriate. It's a zombie. It's not your brother anymore."

"I'm perfectly aware that he's not a person. But he is my brother, and I know they'll have a cure. Maybe not today, maybe not tomorrow, but there will be one and I'll change him back to the way he was." Heinrich's voice was sad, desperate.

"Where are you getting the bodies to feed him?"

Heinrich's eyes widened. "I can't tell you that."

"Do you find them? They have to have died recently, otherwise zombies aren't interested." Elisabeth probed.

"Yeah, sure, I find them." He tried to stuff his hands deeper into his pockets as he spoke, his eyes cast downward.

Elisabeth aimed at the zombie. "Stop lying to me."

"I don't want to lie to you. I just can't tell you the truth. Please, please don't hurt Marcus. He's a good man. He's the one who bit me. It was only an accident, but he didn't kill me! He didn't kill me, so it's only fair that I keep him here until a cure is found," Heinrich begged.

The bullet soared across the room, cleanly ripping through the zombie's skull. It slumped to the floor, meat still clenched in its hand. Heinrich rushed to its side and began to shake it. "No, no, no!" He looked back at Elisabeth, his eyes wet with tears. "There was going to be a cure! He promised! He promised that if I helped him, those people would have to find a way to bring people back from a bite! Marcus, I'm so sorry." He laid the zombie out flat and crossed its arm across its chest. He ran his fingers through its hair lovingly. "I'm so sorry I couldn't save you."

Heinrich walked to the stairs and sat down heavily, holding his face in his hands. "Just a few more weeks. Why did you take him away from me?"

"You were killing innocent people to feed him," Elisabeth said simply.

"I wasn't. They were brought to me."

"Who brought them?"

Heinrich raked his hands through his hair, disheveling it. "Someone else. A woman. I can't tell you."

"Who promised you there would be a cure?"

"I can't tell you that, either."

Elisabeth was growing frustrated. "The war isn't over, damn it!" she yelled. Heinrich's head snapped up, his attention grasped. "We won't have a country to fight for if people like you and whoever this man is are turning survivors into food for zombies. I'm sorry your brother was turned. I'm not sorry that I killed him."

"Did you ever think that while there are still zombies, you still have a reason to get up every morning? Did you ever think that, with zombies, the focus for researchers will be to create a cure? What will you do when all of the zombies are eliminated? What will the labs do when no zombies are around to study and produce a vaccine?" Heinrich asked tiredly. "They'll go back to trying to cure cancer when the zombie virus is a cancer itself!" He looked at her warily.

"I'll always have a reason to wake up in the morning," Elisabeth said softly, thinking of her sister and mother. "I believe that there will be a cure. We've taken care of polio and the measles, tuberculosis, even the bubonic plague. They worked on a vaccine for years after the Ebola outbreak had subsided. I don't doubt they will stop with the zombie virus. It will be just another shot to give your baby when he's six months old."

"You're so different from her and yet so much the same," Heinrich marveled.

"Who is she?"

"I can't tell you." He pointed to his dead brother, his eyes welling up again. "She won't need to bring me bodies anymore. She'll be relieved."

"When you get a conscience, call me," Elisabeth said, fishing a business card out of her pocket.

Heinrich took the card from her hand and set it beside him without looking at it. "We'll see each other again," he promised grimly.

"WE COULDN'T HEAR everything, but we got the gist," Rhys said angrily. "Why did you leave him?" Seeing his leader's expression, he added, "Ma'am."

"I had to leave him. Sometimes you have no choice."

"No choice?" Rhys echoed.

"Yes, no choice. He's like me. We don't have anything strong enough to hold him and I know we don't have a cell to hold him."

"Seems like we need to work on that," Amelia mused.

"That's not why you left him," Dallas said, watching Elisabeth carefully. "You want him to lead us to the mysterious man and woman."

Rhys' brows shot up his forehead. "Ah," he said. "Smart."

"Yes, thank you for that boast of confidence," Elisabeth retorted. "Let's finish clearing this neighborhood and get back to The Creamery."

THE FIGURE SAW ZRT leave. She had heard the gunshot and discarded the limbs it had removed from the bodies at the morgue. There were still other ways to die that weren't a zombie bite, but few remembered that in these chaotic times as the world still shifted from a war to postwar.

She had been walking to the house from another direction and dropped to lie flat on the ground, hoping the grass would cover her so she wouldn't be seen. To be safe, she crawled on her belly until she could no longer see the black SUV and dusted off her torso as she rose to her feet.

She inserted a key into the lock and entered, stamping her feet on the wooden floor to announce her presence.

"You're back," Heinrich said. His eyes were puffy. "She killed my brother."

"I heard. I'm sorry, Heinrich," she said sincerely. "I never intended for that to happen."

"I wanted to kill her for it," he said darkly.

She patted him on his cheek. "No," she said sweetly. "Elisabeth is not to be touched."

"If you love her so much, then why do you protect her?"

"What I'm doing *is* protecting her," she insisted. "There's always a bigger picture. Open your eyes. Can't you see it?"

"I hope Marcus' sacrifice won't be in vain," Heinrich said, his voice cracking.

"Don't be melodramatic. Marcus never had to sacrifice anything. He was infected long before we started."

"You're just as uncaring as Elisabeth!" snapped Heinrich.

"I'm just trying to keep things in their proper perspective. It's called being rational." Seeing Heinrich's pain, she took his hands into her own. "We'll give Marcus a proper burial. Then we'll finish what we started."

ELEVEN

Smoke was streaming lazily out of the chimneys at The Creamery. Bodies were stacked against the walls of the crematorium, the cleanup crew in their usual white hazmat suits. Their supervisor, a larger man with a round belly and thinning hair, greeted the team warmly as they approached. "You're certainly keeping us busy!" Chick Griswold said, his cheeks red from the heat.

Elisabeth looked at the pile of undead. "These aren't ours," she said.

"I was encompassing all of the response teams," Chick clarified. "Luke and the boys took these out late this morning."

"Another outbreak?" Dallas asked.

Chick looked at the undead and quickly counted. "There aren't enough here to be considered the O word. No, these are the ones they took down from the calls they received. That phone was ringing off the hook! I think dispatch could use some more people."

"They can handle themselves just fine," Rhys said.

"I didn't mean anything against them, especially your girl-friend. Glad you all finally decided to go public. Got tired of seeing you sneak in face time back here." Chick grinned and elbowed Rhys playfully.

Rhys blushed while the rest of the team laughed. "Didn't do it that often," he muttered.

"Depends on what your definition of that word is!" Chick replied.

"Did they get all of these at separate locations or were there groups?" Elisabeth was careful to not say "outbreak."

Chick scratched his chin thoughtfully. "Maybe two or three at each place. Nothing they couldn't handle. That Luke sure is a spitfire, isn't he?"

"Oh, he's something," Amelia said, smiling to herself.

An oven door creaked open and the tray pulled out. A crewman swept off the ashes and bones to be ground down into a fine powder. She didn't notice the bones right away and cried out in shock when she touched the hardened calcium.

"Dagnabit, I wish they'd tell these new guys that bones don't always burn down. Too hard or something. That's the whole reason we have to use the grinder! Poor gal, she got a shock, didn't she? I've got to go talk to her. Always great seeing you!" Chick flashed a grin and trotted off to speak to his new crew member.

"Does anyone else find it odd that we had hordes of zombies and now there are small groups of them? It's like it's the same person behind it, but they're trying to be more cautious," Dallas said.

Elisabeth was nodding. "I was thinking the same thing," she agreed.

"Think our friend in quarantine might know anything about this?" Amelia asked.

"Maybe," Elisabeth murmured. She led them to Todd Wilkins' cell where she found him lying in bed, his back to them. "Get up, Todd, we need to talk again."

He didn't move.

"Todd."

Dallas kicked the foot of the bed. Still no movement.

Elisabeth leaned forward. He was dead, but not for very long. She checked for marks and found nothing.

"What happened? How did he die?" Rhys asked.

"Poison," Amelia answered. She was holding up a soda can and pointing to a tiny pinprick near the top. She hesitated. "He's going to come back. The poison just escalated his change. I don't know how long it will be until he wakes up and he'll be hungry for a live buffet."

Elisabeth eyed the needles in her wrist cuff and swore. They were useless against a circulatory system that wasn't working. Her eyes brightened. "Call Chick. Get him down here. We'll put a muzzle on him and tie his hands and feet in case he reanimates. Let Chick throw him into The Creamery."

"I know what he did to you was awful, but that's too violent. He hasn't turned yet. He was still human. He deserves more respect than that," Dallas said reproachfully.

"Let's bind you and turn you into a science project and you can let us know how you feel about it," Amelia snapped. She smiled at Elisabeth. "I think that's an excellent idea."

Rhys was already on the radio. "Chick, we've got another present for you."

ELISABETH PARKED HER car at the old high school she and her team had cleared a few days prior. She had relieved the watchers from observing Heinrich Denis. Headlights sped past her and she got out of her car. The air was crisp, the stars bright, and she began to gently stretch her legs.

Feeling ready, she started out in a light jog, keeping her breathing under control. She picked up her pace after five minutes and soon found herself back at *Quail Hollow*. As her breathing grew heavier, she pushed away her discomfort and thought about what IT had recovered from the audio of the former mayor's cell. He had been talking to himself, but it was mostly gibberish.

"We'll show them why we need the zombies!" he had been whispering. That was the only understood line and Ethan had discredited it. It had come from a desperate man with absolutely nothing left to lose in life. He assumed Todd Wilkins had merely been trying to throw them off.

It still bothered her that there had been another breach in their system and his death had not been recorded. It hadn't even recorded her team trying to speak to him afterward, nor Chick's removal of the body. Ethan had nearly blown a gasket over it and Valerie calmed him, her voice low and smooth.

She ran past several homes and slowed as she approached the end of the subdivision. She ran up the hill to a tree line that separated the subdivision's property from farmland. There were three crosses she could make out in the dark, one in front of a fresh mound of dirt. She shook her head and felt a pang of guilt. She knew this fresh grave must belong to Heinrich's brother. She could have been more understanding. Her own twin probably would have done the same had she not turned into an Abnormal. Thankfully, she knew her mother would have put her out of her misery and from being a danger to others. Love really was a funny thing and chaos was the ultimate test. A lot of people had died at the beginning of the war simply because they refused to believe that their loved ones were dead. They thought that, somewhere deep inside the flesh-eating corpse, the real person remained.

There was faint, flickering light coming from Heinrich's home and Elisabeth strained to see through the windows. Most had the drapes drawn, but the kitchen was like watching a television screen. She saw shadows pass by the window several times as Heinrich walked around his living room. The light suddenly was extinguished and she pressed herself closer against the side of a poplar. The sound of a garage door opening was almost deafening in the silence and Elisabeth watched her target leave in an older station wagon.

She sat down and bit the bottom of her lip, thinking. There was no way she could follow him. He'd see her shadow running down the hill, and despite her special abilities, speed was not one of them. She'd have to wait for him to return. She drew her knees to her chest to fend off the dropping temperature and waited.

Minutes ticked by, turning into an hour. Another hour lapsed and Elisabeth stood, her bones cracking in protest. She stretched

once more, and as she began to step away from the tree line, headlights pierced the darkness. The garage door opened and Heinrich's
station wagon disappeared inside it.

He relit the candles in his home and Elisabeth watched the
shadows. They were erratic, as if he wasn't alone. She heard scuffling
and a scream that was suddenly cut off. Elisabeth darted down the
hill and smashed through the back door, glass shattering around her.
She rolled to her feet and immediately flew back as a heavy fist connected with her jaw.

Jaw aching, she jumped to her feet, her fists raised. The candle-
light was almost too much after spending hours in the dark, but her
eyes adjusted quickly. Heinrich rushed her again and she blocked his
jab, countering with a left hook. She didn't stop with one punch and
continued throwing blows into his stomach. He doubled over in pain,
and she grabbed him by his waist and drove him against the wall. The
sheet rock buckled at the impact and they crashed through into the
dining room.

Stunned, Heinrich was still on his back while she scooted backward, holding onto his left leg. She wrapped her arm around his foot
so that only his heel was poking out and she pulled. Heinrich yelled
with pain as the tendons in his knees popped. Elisabeth released his
foot and straddled his stomach, widening her legs so that her weight
felt even heavier. She grabbed his head and began slamming it into
the floor until he fell unconscious.

A sniffle caught her attention and she looked up, a little startled
to see several people tied to the dining room chairs. She looked down
at the bloody face of Heinrich and back at them. Slowly, she stood up
and tried to brush off the sheet rock dust from her clothes. Sheepishly, she waved.

"Hello," she croaked, her throat coated with dust. "I promise I'm
one of the good guys."

HEINRICH DENIS WOKE to find himself handcuffed to a steel support beam in his basement. He tried to break free of the cuffs and was surprised when the restraints didn't budge.

"Titanium handcuffs," Elisabeth said. "They won't last forever, but they'll do for now. You'll have to thank Amelia for those."

Heinrich glared at her and she flashed a smile. He could hear others moving around upstairs, but said nothing.

"I hope you don't mind that I invited the rest of my team into your home, along with an ambulance." Her eyes narrowed. "What were you doing with those people?"

Heinrich spat. "You ungrateful bitch," he snapped.

Elisabeth punched him. "I'm not in the mood for this, Heinrich. What is it that I'm missing?"

"This is all for you. All of it. Even after you killed poor Marcus, I still want the same thing: I want a cure."

"If there are enough zombies, there will be a vaccine developed."

"Yes."

"How is this for me? How does this help me? I like being an Abnormal. It makes me better at my job."

"This helps you *keep* your job. This helps you not wind up as a lab rat."

"I don't even know you!" Elisabeth said, exasperated.

Heinrich was suddenly calm. "This wasn't my plan. This was *their* plan."

"Who are they? What plan?" Elisabeth demanded.

"He just wanted to do tests. She wanted to keep you safe. Infect a few people, drop them here and there, stir the pot so to speak, and they both get what they want." Heinrich laughed softly. "They never even knew about each other, but their goals were similar, and I just wanted my brother back."

"How did you meet them if they don't know each other?"

"Out." His jaw clenched.

Elisabeth was quiet for a few moments, absorbing the information. "Who are they?" she asked again.

Heinrich stuck out his chin defiantly. "I told you already that I can't tell you. This is all for your best interests, though."

Elisabeth pointed at the ceiling. "What about those people upstairs? Where did you find them? What were you going to do with them?"

"I found them here and there. I was going to turn them. For everyone. For you."

"Because these people told you to."

"Yes."

Elisabeth unlocked the handcuffs long enough to remove him from the support beam. She relocked them and shoved him forward. He limped heavily on his good leg; the tendons in his other leg were still healing. He took the stairs one at a time, wincing with each step.

Outside, the people he had kidnapped shrunk at the sight of him and he smiled mirthlessly. "You'll find out everything soon enough," he promised. "I won't stay in jail for too long."

Elisabeth ignored him and guided him to the company's SUV. As they passed the group, he suddenly lunged forward and tried to bite an elderly woman. The woman shrieked and fainted, Amelia catching her effortlessly.

As if in slow motion, Elisabeth saw one of the emergency medical technicians raise his gun and pull the trigger. "No!" she shouted. "The blood!"

It was too late. Warm blood splashed across her face and the others nearby as Heinrich's head exploded. Instantly she could smell the infection spreading. She stood for a beat, too stunned to move.

"Which ones?" Amelia asked, appearing at Elisabeth's side.

"All of them. The EMTs included."

"Our team?"

"Nothing passed the membranes."

Amelia made a swirling motion with her finger, the team already reaching into their wrist cuffs. Needles were being plunged into skin with soft, soothing words of encouragement that everything would be okay.

Elisabeth stared at Heinrich's body and frowned. Suddenly, everything clicked into place. "He wanted this to happen."

"I don't think he wanted his head blown off, ma'am," Rhys said.

"No. He wanted to infect these people."

HEINRICH'S HOUSE WAS empty, the front yard covered in blood stains and footprints. The woman stood in the doorway with her hands on her hips and shook her head. She had warned him ZRT would be watching him. He had called her the night before, so happy that he had found a family hiding out in a bomb shelter. She berated him for not infecting them immediately. "We could have moved them after," she snapped. Heinrich had apologized and said that he was lonely with Marcus gone, and while no one could replace his brother, he had wanted the people at his house for the company.

Her heels clacked loudly against the hardwood floors as she walked to the kitchen. She had liked Heinrich and mourned his loss, though she realized that she felt a little relieved that he was gone. She had already disposed of the mayor, and she thought about removing the judge as well, but decided his role should merely be to keep ZRT on their toes. That and, without Heinrich, it would be difficult to take him on her own. He had already secured the last area and everything was ready. She just had to be patient for a few more days.

She looked underneath the sink and found paper bags. Not wanting food to go to waste, she rummaged through Heinrich's cabinets, silently thanking him for being so generous to her. She felt guilty that he had been taken to The Creamery and that he wouldn't be buried next to his family, but he had died for the cause just like everyone else they had taken. She thought about the future and, feeling hopeful, began to hum.

TWELVE

"**E**than, it's not one of us." Elisabeth's gaze was steady as the director's face went from surprise to fury to confusion.

The other teams had gathered in the conference room, Valerie leaning against a cabinet in the corner. Her blonde hair was in soft waves around her face, a stark contrast against her navy-blue suit. Initially, she had asked Ethan if she could return to her office in Nashville, but Ethan had refused, saying he might need her again for another press conference. Now Pine Valley was growing on her, and she was enjoying some of her time spent with Dallas Anderson and his father in the evenings. Hugh Anderson was a card shark and she would have been broke if they had been playing with real money. She felt guilty for hoping that she wasn't becoming too attached.

Valerie listened as a murmur erupted amongst the men and women, though Team Mayfair was quiet. Elisabeth had more of an open book policy with her team than the other leaders, something Valerie admired. She liked watching Elisabeth work, the way her brow knitted together in concentration. She handled herself well under pressure and her team adored her. She was sure they'd follow her to hell itself if she asked. She had met Elisabeth's twin sister, Margo, and they had lunch together the previous afternoon. She hadn't realized her sister was a reporter and had been standing in the back of the room during the press conference Valerie had held, but she chalked it up to flashing cameras obscuring her vision. Margo was different from her twin, though it was clear that she loved her dearly. They had discussed fashion and Valerie had promised a shopping trip should Margo ever find herself in Nashville. She never asked why Valerie left the White House, and Valerie appreciated that. For a reporter, the woman certainly didn't pry. She had seemed a little distracted, though she been discreet about it and Valerie didn't ask. She, too, hadn't wanted to pry.

"What the hell? You thought one of us was killing all of those people and dumping them throughout town?" someone asked from Teach Churchill.

Elisabeth said nothing, letting the director of Division Tennessee flounder. Valerie smiled despite herself. She respected Ethan, but he needed to have more faith in his response teams.

The director's mouth opened and closed before finally speaking. "Yes, we thought it was a team member, but clearly we were wrong." He inhaled, his breath uneven. "We haven't had an outbreak in ages and here we are, faced with several in a small amount of time. We have to assume the worst." He hung his head, and Valerie caught his eye and smiled. Ethan had been sincere with his words, but Valerie had made him practice actually looking the part as well.

The director continued, "We believe Heinrich Denis was the mayor's partner. He wanted to find a cure for his now-deceased brother, and we believe he was the one who had agreed to supply the individuals for study. We also know he was helping a woman spread the infection, though for what purpose we are unsure."

Apologize to your teams, Valerie thought.

Ethan sighed deeply, struggling to find his next words. "I'm sorry for doubting your intentions. The truth is that everyone here is a fine employee and I couldn't ask for anyone better."

Rhys elbowed the director in the ribs. "We accept your apology, sir, and we won't tell anyone else that you like us the most." He winked.

The mood lighter, Elisabeth seemed satisfied.

"Valerie and I will be leaving tomorrow. You all can finish sorting the rest of this mess without our presence," Ethan said.

Dallas leaned forward and rested on his elbows. He was frowning. "Wait. Why infect all of those people and send them out around town? In caves, no less?"

"This area is riddled with caves that serve as an easy access point to the public. You create outbreaks, you create panic. You create a need for an illegal lab and maybe no one will question what you're doing or how you're doing it because they're too desperate," Ethan answered smoothly. "As for this woman, I expect you to find her and eliminate her. However, don't expect to find someone who is sane. This might be a person who wanted chaos for the sake of chaos."

"We still don't know who killed Todd Wilkins and who shut down the cameras," Dallas said pointedly.

"That's still under investigation."

Dallas nodded, but Valerie could tell he wasn't content with the director's response. The man had a lousy poker face. She glanced at the rest of Team Mayfair and they, too, seemed uneasy. She knew Ethan wasn't worrying about cameras or the mayor's death. He had made sure IT had fixed their system so that it was impenetrable, and while he had been furious that someone had infiltrated it, he wasn't too concerned that the person had done what they were going to have to do anyway. In his eyes, it was clearly someone at ZRT and it was sort of a mercy killing rather than making the man wait for the inevitable.

Oblivious to Dallas' reaction, Ethan continued, "I understand there's a celebration this evening. This matter has been taken care of thanks to you all, and the Appalachian Caverns is opening to the public after many years of being shuttered." He nodded his head toward Elisabeth. "I understand we've cleared the area and they'd like to invite us to their grand opening ceremony as a way to say their thanks." He smiled broadly. "I'll see you all there, I'm sure," he said before excusing himself.

The teams remained in the conference room as Ethan went into the hall and toward his temporary office. Valerie matched his step and they walked in silence. He sat behind his desk and began clearing papers into a briefcase as Valerie shut the door.

"You're leaving open some loose ends with them, don't you think?" she asked.

"Of course I am," he replied simply.

"Why? What's the purpose of that?"

"Their job is to respond to calls of duress from zombie attacks. They handle the issue and they move on to the next call."

Valerie crossed her arms. "There's no reason to not tell these people everything. Just tell them the truth about IT fixing the issue and that you're not actually investigating who removed the mayor."

"I'm not going to do that. They don't need to think they can murder someone and not suffer the consequences," the director snapped.

"I understand," Valerie said slowly, careful to not push too hard. "There are, however, some cases where transparency is the key to a trusting and effective unit. You could at least tell them that their security system has been repaired and they shouldn't have any other problems."

Ethan grumbled. "You're right, I should have told them that. I will. I'll have IT send out an email."

"That's the way to be hands-on," Valerie said sarcastically.

The director sighed and rubbed his hands over his face. He suddenly looked very tired. "I'm doing the best that I can. We're lucky these outbreaks and illegal lab are an isolated incident. The other directors are on alert, but everything has been calm. It's like the Second Reconstruction for our country right now. We can't handle another wave of undead. We *will* fall and I don't know if we could survive it." He looked at her warily. "Even your kind."

Valerie uncrossed her arms and leaned forward to put her hand on his forearm. "You're just a big softie inside."

"Don't tell anyone."

SAMANTHA CHAPEL'S FOOTSTEPS were silent as she walked on the Lower Bridge. She held a flashlight in her left hand, but it was turned off thanks to the new lighting system that had been installed. The path was well-lit and everything seemed to be in working order.

She passed one of Atlas' arms and grinned. She loved being in the caverns. The air was heavy and cool, and the sounds of water constantly dripping reminded her of a symphony. Her parents had brought her here as a child, and when she found out the town wanted to reopen it, she jumped at the chance to be on the crew.

There had been a lot of trash and debris they had to remove after years of people using it as a hiding place during the war. The old walkways were cracked and some of the handrails had been torn loose. They had been prepared to find bodies as well, but they had lucked out and found none. Samantha had said a quick prayer after their first sweep because she didn't know how much more death she could handle.

The walkways were smooth now, freshly poured and ready for another generation of feet to cross them. The crew had kept everything looking as natural as possible and the final result was beautiful.

Satisfied with the lights and walkways, she dropped off the path and toward a section of the caverns meant for their Adventure Tour. It was going to be for more experienced spelunkers and she was excited to be one of the guides. She wasn't going to check those particular sections because she didn't have her gear, but there was a place that she considered her favorite spot and it was easy to access from the main trail.

The opening was narrow and a tight squeeze. Samantha almost had to turn sideways to fit and she found it strangely exhilarating. The opening widened and she could breathe more easily. The space was small, the ceiling low. She shone her flashlight above her and the water glittered like stars. She could stay there for hours watching the droplets twinkle and she had used it as an escape during the renovations.

A breeze rustled her hair and she turned, noticing for the first time a second opening. She crossed the small space in a few steps and noticed a large boulder that had previously covered the entrance. She hadn't seen it before because it had blended so well with the wall. Her flashlight bobbed around the tunnel that led away from the space and she was tempted to follow it. She wondered why she hadn't seen it before and decided it had been added at the last minute. She'd have to explore it at a later time so that she'd be able to lead the Adventure Tour groups that way.

Samantha squeezed back through the narrow opening and climbed back up to the walkway. Clicking off her flashlight, she followed the path to the mouth of the caverns. The sun had lowered in the sky and the leaves crunched underneath her shoes. She stopped and turned to look at the caverns with a smile. She hoped they would make everyone as happy as they had made her.

"HOW MANY FOLKS do you expect to be at this opening?" Dallas asked. The team had crowded into Elisabeth's office, despite being the only ones left.

"A lot. Small town. Some place is having a party. Life has been hell. Why not go?" Amelia said.

Rhys nodded in agreement. "Tammy wants to get dressed up." He looked at Elisabeth. "I think she's wearing something your sister let her borrow."

Elisabeth groaned. Margo had so many clothes that a sample rack at a fashion magazine couldn't hold a candle to her collection.

"Anyone else get the impression that the matter Ethan discussed hasn't been resolved? That he doesn't take this mystery woman Heinrich mentioned seriously?" Dallas asked slowly.

"He did tie it up neatly in a bow, didn't he?" Amelia whispered. She pointed to the ceiling. "Someone might be listening."

Elisabeth waved her hand dismissively. "It's not a conspiracy. I do agree with you, though. It adds up too perfectly, almost."

"Maybe that's okay," Rhys interjected. "Sometimes it really can be as simple as that."

"Then who killed Todd?" Dallas asked.

Rhys made a face. "I can't know *every* detail. I bet Valerie did it. She hates violence and all that. She probably just didn't want to see Elisabeth do away with him."

"I was upset that he didn't reanimate after Chick put him in the furnace," Elisabeth admitted unhappily.

"Don't you find it curious that the cameras went out then? That the audio hadn't been working?" Dallas probed.

"A coincidence. Look, guys. It's technology. Technology that's not as good as what we had prewar. It's going to be faulty." Rhys held out his hands, palms up. "Let's go to this opening. The owners invited us specifically. The town needs it. *We* need it."

"You just want to show off your relationship that is now public." Amelia laughed.

"Guilty," Rhys admitted. "We have a new role-playing game now," he began.

"That's enough," Elisabeth interrupted. "I'll take into consideration what Ethan said, but I think we'll still be on the lookout for any other instances that seem out of the ordinary. This woman might not be able to infect others on her own and that's why she needed Heinrich. If that's the case, then she might be done and no longer a threat. If we see another group that has more than three, we'll know we still have a problem."

"We still get to bring our guns to this thing, right?" Amelia asked.

"Absolutely."

APPALACHIAN CAVERNS WAS crowded with hundreds of Pine Valley citizens. Samantha Chapel beamed and she looked at Nancy and Frederick Carter, the owners. They were chatting excitedly with one of the mayoral candidates. Everyone was dressed in such lovely clothes and Samantha felt herself swelling with pride. It reminded her of a fancy opening for a new exhibit at the Museum of Natural History in New York City. The gift shop was filled to capacity with patrons perusing the shelves and the others were milling about the grounds, carefree and happy.

She spotted one of the ZRT members and waved vigorously before threading her way through the crowd. "Hi!" she said brightly. "I'm so glad that you could come!"

Elisabeth Mayfair smiled and shook her hand. "Thanks for the special invitation." As she spoke, her fellow teammates joined them. "Samantha Chapel, please meet my sister, Margo, and my mother, Ruth. That's Hugh, Dallas' father."

"So lovely to meet you, young lady," Hugh Anderson said, lightly kissing the back of Samantha's hand.

"Ah, this is Tammy, our office manager," Elisabeth continued.

"And my girlfriend," Rhys added. His chest was puffed out and Samantha caught Amelia discreetly trying to roll her eyes.

"When are the tours?" Ruth asked. She was wringing her hands. "I can't wait to go! I feel like I get so cooped up in the house."

"In just a few minutes," Samantha promised. "I'll lead you myself."

"Did you know there's a secret entrance?" Hugh asked mysteriously.

Samantha nodded. "Oh, yes. We sealed that yesterday."

"You did?" Margo asked. She looked disappointed.

"We decided one point of ingress and egress was best for our Adventure Tours."

Hugh's face fell. He had wanted to share the story again. Seeing this, Samantha said, "I'm sure you can tell me other things about this area." He brightened and launched into a quick history lesson.

When he was finished, Samantha thanked him and excused herself so that she could greet others who had arrived.

"What a nice girl," Hugh said admirably. "Kids these days need to know their history."

"Dad, she's probably in her early forties."

"Still a kid to me, son."

"Everyone! May I please have your attention?" Samantha was shouting so that her voice would carry over the crowd. Immediately everyone was quiet and she continued. "We have a few guides here, including myself. We're going to get into groups of fifteen and start the tours!"

The crowd cheered and Samantha held up her hands to silence them.

"I'm going to begin this evening and may I please have the following people join my group?" She ticked off names, and as they were called, people gathered around her.

Elisabeth watched as her team's family members surrounded Samantha, along with a few others she didn't recognize, but assumed were important. "Sorry," Samantha said as she passed Elisabeth. "You'll get to tour later. We kind of figured that you all have already seen it." Elisabeth smiled politely. She secretly hoped that her sister and mother could go inside, see everything, and then they could leave. She wasn't fond of crowds.

Team Mayfair watched as another group followed Samantha's ten minutes later. They saw Teams Aguilar and Churchill, both unsuccessfully avoiding the director and his mouthpiece. Elisabeth understood. She liked Ethan and Valerie, but having the boss in town was nerve-wracking.

Amelia was called for the next group. "See you later, suckers," she said. "Guess I get to go home first tonight!"

"I'm really proud of you all," Ethan said awkwardly. He had taken Elisabeth off to the side, near the mouth of the caverns. "Your team does excellent work."

"So do Aguilar and Churchill," Elisabeth said.

"Yes, and I thanked them already. Glad this problem is all but gone."

Suddenly, a scream pierced the crowd.

Stunned, everyone froze. Like a river, the previous tour groups began spilling out into the opening. Their cries ripped through the air, causing a stampede of people trying to run away from something that no one else could see yet.

Calmly, Amelia strolled out. She saw her team leader. "Let's get those guns you wanted us to bring."

"Zombies? Here?" Ethan asked, surprised.

"Nope, we just thought we'd screw with you a little." Amelia pointed her finger toward Ethan. "And this is the director. Can we get those guns now?"

"Already on it!" Rhys and Dallas were dragging a trunk behind them. Tammy followed, struggling to keep up as her heels sank into the earth. "I told you not to wear those stupid things to a cave," Rhys admonished her.

"Margo said they went with the dress!"

"Where's our family?" Dallas demanded, looking at Amelia.

Amelia pointed west. "I told Hugh and Ruth to get back to their cars." She hesitated. "I didn't see your sister."

Samantha stumbled over her feet as she ran to Elisabeth. "Your sister went down the tunnel! She's gone! I'm so sorry! She's gone! She was so excited that she cut ahead of me and the next thing I knew, she was gone!" Samantha was sobbing.

"You went off the path?" Elisabeth asked.

"She asked for it!" Samantha cried.

"Where did you go?" Elisabeth demanded.

Samantha quickly answered and Elisabeth's gaze flickered to the caverns.

Zombies began shambling out of the mouth of the cave. There were a few at first, then more began to pour out.

"Tammy, Samantha, direct these people away from here. Everyone else, grab a weapon and get with the other teams."

"We brought our own!" Luke Aguilar boasted. "Thought we might see some action." His team was already passing out their guns and rifles.

"You expected this to happen?" Ethan was in disbelief.

"Too neat of a bow," Amelia muttered.

Ethan reached for the Ruger AR-556 and Dallas stared at him. "That's mine, director," he said, snatching it out of the director's hands.

"Nothing for you, I see," Valerie said thoughtfully, appearing next to Elisabeth.

"That means more for everyone else."

Valerie scowled at her deep purple dress and black cashmere cardigan. "I knew I should've worn something else." She reached down and tore off the bottom of her dress so that her legs weren't restricted.

"I thought you didn't like violence."

"I don't. I also don't want to see people getting killed."

Elisabeth said nothing. She turned and darted into the caverns, gunshots ringing out around her as the teams tried to staunch the flow of the undead.

Inside the cave, zombies crowded on the walkway. A few had gone off the path and were eating some of the people who had gone on the tour first.

"Poor bastards never stood a chance," Valerie said behind her.

The women punched and shoved their way through, taking out zombies along the way. Elisabeth saw the turn off where Samantha said she had taken her group and hopped over the handrail.

"I'll stay here, see if I can't get rid of anymore." Valerie gasped. She grabbed the back of a zombie's neck and yanked out its brain stem. Elisabeth's eyebrows shot up in surprise. "Don't tell Ethan," Valerie yelled. Then she was plowing through the throng of undead and Elisabeth could no longer see her.

The stream of zombies was getting slower as Elisabeth approached the spot Samantha had taken her group. She easily dispatched them, though she wished she had grabbed a stick or just *anything* at this point. Her knuckles ached and she knew she had bone fragments sticking out of her skin.

At the entrance, Elisabeth realized why there were less zombies. The opening was very narrow and the zombie she was staring at was extraordinarily fat. It was stuck, though the swarm behind it was piling up and pushing against it. It moved slightly, howling as it struggled to move out of the way.

An explosion rang out and shook the walls around her. Chunks fell from the ceiling and Elisabeth whirled back toward the entrance. It hadn't come from that direction. Puzzled, she threw her body against the stuck zombie, trying to get past it. The pressure of her body against it and the other zombies from the other side was too much. Elisabeth sensed what was about to happen and ducked out of the way as the zombie's stomach burst. Its contents had nowhere to go and rained back down on top of the zombies, the smell enough to make Elisabeth feel like she needed to vomit.

She was desperate. She wanted to get to her sister, hopefully save her, but she couldn't let this chance of a bottleneck pass. A stalactite had broken free from the explosion and Elisabeth grabbed it, grateful to have a weapon. She pierced the stuck zombie's skull and yanked it out of the way. With her stalactite, she punctured heads as the undead filed through the opening.

She could still hear shots from the entrance and knew the teams had to be running low on ammo. They had Valerie, at least, and Elisabeth pressed onward, now past the opening. More zombies were coming through the tunnel and she destroyed them, cursing when her makeshift weapon finally crumbled in her grip. Still holding a small piece, she used it like a rock and smashed it against hard bone. Skulls caved inward, zombies collapsed, and Elisabeth continued onward.

Further down the tunnel she went, not recognizing it from the last time she and her team had been there. She frowned, realizing they had missed an entire tunnel after she heard her teammates call for her and she had had to dive into the lake.

Hand raised holding the rock, she moved forward, ready to strike. The caverns were loaded with so many zombies that her senses were overloaded and she couldn't tell if there were any more where she was going. She feared the worst for her sister and pushed the thought out of her head. "Margo!" she called.

No reply came and Elisabeth wished she had a flashlight. It was pitch black as she walked blindly through the tunnel. She used her other hand as a guide, the wall rough and damp.

To her bewilderment, a small amount of moonlight was poking through ahead. Now *this* she did recognize. It was the second entrance, though the hole was bigger than she remembered. She looked around the chamber and noticed the other exits had been blocked. There were several shackles and ropes here.

Elisabeth swore. Someone had come in after they cleared it and planted the infected. She should have sealed the other entrance then, and she chided herself for not doing so.

The seal the crew at Appalachian Caverns had put in place had clearly been blown. Elisabeth saw the ragged edges and bits of crumbled concrete on the ground. She dug her fingers into the side of the wall and began to climb, struggling because the wall curved and she was almost upside down when she reached the opening.

Fingernails ripping off, Elisabeth pulled herself out of the cavern and looked around, the black bear she had encountered flashing across her mind. There was a small trail of blood and she followed it, straining to see in the pale moonlight.

She heard heavy breathing and stopped, ears trying to pinpoint the location. She turned and saw a figure slumped against a tree. Even a normal nose could smell the amount of blood in the air.

Elisabeth rushed to the figure and stopped suddenly, shocked.

THIRTEEN

"**M**argo!" she cried, relief flooding through her. Margo tried to sit up straighter, but wound up slumping down further. Her skin was burned, her hands badly shredded from clawing her way out of the caverns. She was bleeding severely from her abdomen and Elisabeth pressed her hand firmly over the wound.

Fighting back tears, Elisabeth told her, "You're going to be okay. It's going to be okay. We'll get you out of here."

Margo opened her mouth to speak, but blood poured out instead.

"No, no, you're going to be fine!" Elisabeth said, trying to remain calm for her sister.

Margo grabbed Elisabeth's forearm and struggled to speak. Elisabeth shook her head, telling her to be quiet. "I need to tell you the truth," Margo gurgled.

"Shut up," Elisabeth begged.

"I did this," Margo admitted.

"I don't know how you got a bomb, but I'm glad you got out of there. You're going to be okay," Elisabeth reaffirmed.

"Elisabeth." Margo caught her sister's gaze. "I don't have a bite on me."

"No, you got lucky. You—" Elisabeth cut herself off, her eyes widening. "How?" she asked, confused.

"I told you that some places had come up with ways to dye the irises."

"I still don't understand. Why would you do this?"

"Heinrich helped me at first. Then that company came along and I let him infect me. We share the same DNA. I hoped that would be enough. Then I became a shallow client," Margo explained weakly.

Her hands still keeping pressure on her sister's wound, Elisabeth demanded, "Why? Why would you do that to all of those people?"

"For you. To keep you safe. I didn't want anyone to hurt you. I wanted ZRT to have a reason to need you, to keep you out of their labs. I didn't want them to do anything to you."

Elisabeth stared at her sister, stunned. When she spoke, her voice was thick. "They'll always need me for something. They won't put me in a lab against my will."

"Don't be stupid, Elisabeth. There aren't that many Abnormals and they'll take you. The way the mayor tried to take you." Margo laughed softly. "I told you I didn't like that man."

"You killed Todd," Elisabeth said slowly.

"I did it for you. I didn't know he and Heinrich had a side deal going, and when I found out, I disabled the cameras."

"What about the audio before then?"

Margo looked at her sister, a brief flash of annoyance crossing her face. "That really was a glitch. Older standards produce older results. I disabled the cameras, but no one questioned me when I was there."

"They thought you were me."

"I didn't actually see anyone when I went to quarantine, but even the mayor thought that I was you."

"Margo, I can't forgive you for this. You murdered innocent people."

Margo smiled sadly. "I tried to keep you safe. You kept Mom and me alive during the war. You still do. I wanted to repay you. I wanted to protect you." Her breathing was becoming shallow.

"Hang on, Margo!" Elisabeth begged. The blast had wounded Margo more than her healing could keep up with, and she was pale from blood loss. She passed out, her head resting on her chest. Elisabeth picked up her sister and threw her over her shoulder. She ran as quickly as she could, hoping she was on the same path Amelia had taken previously when she discovered the second entrance.

"Please, please don't die on me," Elisabeth pleaded. Her sister remained unconscious.

LOW ON AMMUNITION, Teams Aguilar and Churchill stayed in their positions, trying to remove the horde that was now out of the caverns completely.

"Damn it, shoot them in the head!" Luke shouted.

Ethan grunted in response. "Been a while since I've been out in the field."

Most of the crowd had dispersed, Amelia and Rhys pulling up the rear to remove any threats. Dallas could hear them returning, hoping the others had gotten far enough away that the zombies were only interested in the humans who were still on site.

"Fuck, I'm out!" Nicholas yelled.

Valerie ran toward them, her hair disheveled and clothes torn. Blood caked her skin and some gray brain matter had embedded itself into the folds of her dress. "Knives!" Dallas and Luke handed her their large Bowie knives.

She was like a tornado, whirling around and slicing through the brain stems like butter. Zombies fell in piles around her and she was onto the next bunch, stabbing and piercing.

Those without bullets joined those who still did, acting as lookouts. Amelia had joined them, her face expressionless as she fired shot after shot. Rhys' teeth were gritted as he aimed, killed, and repeated.

Dallas ran out and rummaged through the trunk, hoping to find more ammunition. "Is this a crossbow?"

"Yeah," Amelia said.

"You packed a damn crossbow?"

"Yeah," Amelia repeated.

"You did it because *Buffy the Vampire Slayer* used one, didn't you?" he asked.

"Um. Yes. Yes, I did."

Dallas shrugged. "Okay, then." He carefully aimed and fired, the bolt soaring through the air. It landed in a zombie's shoulder.

"Oh, for fuck's sake, switch with me," Amelia said, annoyed. She traded weapons and reloaded the crossbow quickly. She pulled the trigger and the bolt plowed through a zombie's ear. It dropped immediately.

"I just needed a couple of shots to warm up," Dallas argued.

"I'm sure you did, buddy," Rhys said, his voice strained.

The horde was thinning, but a quick count told Dallas they weren't going to last that long.

Elisabeth appeared out of nowhere and dropped her sister carefully to the ground. "Keep pressure on that wound! Don't get the blood on you!" she ordered. Nicholas pulled rubber gloves out of the small first aid kit in the weapons trunk and placed his hands over Margo's stomach. Luke ripped fabric from the bottom of Amelia's dress for makeshift bandages.

She grabbed a rifle. "It's out," Rhys said.

"Not a problem." Elisabeth held it like a baseball bat and began swinging as hard as she could. Heads rolled and she remembered the gym, choking back tears at the thought of her sister being the cause of those deaths.

Valerie ran past her, throwing one of her Bowie knives. She was screaming with rage. The knife sunk into the back of a skull and she stopped, ripped it out, and continued with her rampage.

Ammunition depleted, the teams remained in place. Elisabeth ordered them to retreat and her team fled, carrying Margo with them to their car.

"We stay until the end," Luke Aguilar said, determined. A zombie shambled up behind him and Elisabeth swung, Luke ducking out of the way. "I suppose you two don't need our help after all." He motioned for his team to leave and they followed him. Team Churchill was already gone.

Elisabeth's rifle broke and she stooped over to grab another. Valerie was moving quickly, her knives deadly as more zombies dropped. There weren't many left and Elisabeth sat on the ground, exhaustion sweeping over her. She watched as Valerie finished the last few, her chest heaving as she caught her breath.

Valerie dropped the knives and sank to the ground next to Elisabeth. Suddenly, she looked around sheepishly. "How much of that do you think Ethan saw?"

TWO DAYS LATER, Elisabeth stared at her sister, her gut twisted. Somehow, she and Todd Wilkins had both met Heinrich Denis. Margo had wanted to keep her sister safe from becoming a laboratory experiment and had asked Heinrich to infect others. She had told him that, with new hordes created and attacking, scientists would be scrambling to come up with a cure and they could fix his brother. It was a win-win situation for them both. She'd even gambled on letting him infect her, turning her into an Abnormal as well. To hide her eye color, she had them dyed and Elisabeth snickered at the lengths her sister went through to hide her condition. Todd had also wanted to find a cure and, selfishly, a way to enhance himself. He just wasn't willing to be as ethical about finding the results. Heinrich had decided to help them both by spreading the virus and by providing bodies, both infected and not, hoping it would increase the chances of returning Marcus to his former self.

Margo was lying peacefully in the hospital bed, monitors beeping and chirping. The doctors had said she was healing much faster than they expected, and were confident in her full recovery. Relieved, their mother had finally left her side to get something to eat.

The director had returned to Nashville. Valerie had requested to stay behind for a few more days and Elisabeth knew it was to say goodbye properly to Dallas. If he got his wish, she'd stay in Pine Valley.

Elisabeth had lied to Ethan. She had lied to everyone and it gnawed on her conscience. She had told them that she had found her sister hidden in a corner, the zombies miraculously never sensing her nearby. It was Elisabeth who had blown away the seal for her and Margo to escape, and though Margo had suffered greatly because of it, she had seen no better way to protect her sister. She had said that Heinrich removed the seal with his great strength, dumped in the infected, and replaced it. Everyone bought her story. There was no reason not to. She had never lied to them.

The ZRT cleanup crew had to call in reinforcements to collect all of the bodies. Chick Griswold had had a field day because of it. Ethan agreed to quarantine almost a hundred infected people from the attack, giving them a chance to say their goodbyes.

All of the teams were busy with their reports and helping Tammy set up relative visits for the infected. It was a huge mess and Elisabeth found herself staring angrily at Margo.

She remained quiet for a long while, contemplating her next move. Slowly, she rose and leaned over her sister. Whispering into her ear, she said, "I love you. I love you more than you'll ever know. What you did was wrong. Horrible. You're a murderess. I will *never* forgive you. Don't mistake my covering for you as weakness. I will be keeping a close eye on you and don't doubt me for a minute when I say that I *will* kill you myself if I have to. Consider this your one pass because you're my twin and I understand why you did it." Her voice grew hard. "Don't test me."

Elisabeth straightened and left the hospital room.

Margo opened her eyes and watched her sister leave. She shuddered at her sister's warning. "I promise," she said softly.

EPILOGUE

"**D**ad, there's a zombie!" Farrah Ellis tugged on the bottom of her father's jacket.

"Shush, honey, I almost got this," Neville Ellis said. He raised his ax to swing again and the tree fell to its side.

"Dad!" squealed the little girl.

"What?" Neville looked up and saw a couple of zombies wandering through the Berman Christmas Tree Farm. "Oh. Don't worry, honey." He picked her up and noted the location of his tree before heading toward the main office.

"Did you find the perfect tree?" the cashier asked, smiling.

"Sure did," Neville answered. "But we do have a small problem. Saw a couple of zombies milling about. Might want to call ZRT."

"Really? Shoot. Thanks for letting me know!" the cashier said brightly. She punched in a few numbers and a cool female voice answered. She assured the cashier they would have someone there soon and the cashier replaced the phone in its cradle. "Just stay here and they'll be here in a jiff."

The zombies had made it to the main office and began banging on the walls. Farrah began to cry and her father tried to soothe her, though fear was creeping into his voice.

"Christmas tree farms are just weird," Rhys said, eyeing the rows of trees as he pulled into the parking lot. He parked the SUV by the main office and the team hopped out, weapons ready. There were only two zombies, though one had just broken through the glass and was starting to crawl inside.

Amelia fired and the zombie went down. Dallas was already running around to the other side of the building. He had the crossbow and whistled as the bolt went through the back of the second zombie's neck. "You're getting better with that," Amelia commented.

"Thanks!" he replied gratefully, pulling out the bolt from the dead zombie.

"Who'd you get for secret Santa?" Rhys asked quietly.

"I got Dallas. I'm going to get him some more bolts. Who'd you get?"

"I got Elisabeth."

"Good luck with that," Amelia teased.

"Yeah, she's been so moody lately, she gives me whiplash," Rhys replied.

"Don't talk about her sister and you'll be fine," Amelia advised.

"Wonder what happened between them."

"Don't know. Don't ask," Amelia warned.

Elisabeth checked the dead zombies and entered the main office. "Lindsey Rosenburg?" she asked.

The cashier nodded. "That's me."

"You reported a zombie to dispatch eleven minutes ago?"

The cashier glanced at the clock on the wall. "I suppose I did."

"Did any of you have any interaction with the zombies?" Elisabeth asked, already knowing the answer.

"Oh, no," the cashier answered cheerily. "You all were here in the nick of time!"

Elisabeth nodded and called the cleanup crew.

Rhys groaned. "She's going to be impossible to buy for."

"I heard that," Elisabeth said once she hung up the phone. "Get me another 9mm."

"That's outside the budget we all agreed on," Rhys protested.

"Call me impossible again and I'll ask for two." She flashed a smile.

Rhys cleared his throat. "Yes, ma'am!"

ACKNOWLEDGMENTS

Thank you to my family and friends for your enthusiasm and support. I'd also like to extend a special thank you to my beta readers, Isaac and Stephanie Aguilar, for being the first to read *ZRT: Division Tennessee* and giving me honest feedback. You two are true friends.

ABOUT THE AUTHOR

Stephanie Grey is the author of *ZRT: Division Tennessee*, *A Witchly Influence*, and *The Immortal Prudence Blackwood*. Writing has always been her passion, and she enjoys exploring different genres.

Stephanie is a graduate of East Tennessee State University and she holds a degree in journalism. When she's not writing, she enjoys spending time with her husband, Brazilian jiu-jitsu, visiting museums, reading, and playing with her cat. One day she may even turn into a crazy cat lady because nothing in life is interesting without a little bit of crazy.

Lightning Source UK Ltd.
Milton Keynes UK
UKHW010634291021
393035UK00002B/253